CANDLELIGHT

Supreme

"YOU AREN'T AFRAID OF ANYTHING, ARE YOU?" SAMANTHA ASKED, ANNOYED.

"Sure I am. Women like you," Brock replied quickly.

"Women like me? What does that mean?"

"Helpless."

"Helpless! I'll have you know I've been on my own for years and have done very well, Brock Slader."

"Sure, back where you come from you probably have," he admitted. "But here you're totally out of your element."

Samantha couldn't argue with that. The Amazon was as different from New Orleans as she could ever get.

"I'm not a hero, Sam. I don't make a habit of rescuing people," he said quietly.

"Then why did you rescue me yesterday at the hotel? You could have ignored me. Why, Brock?" she demanded.

"I don't know." He smiled wryly. "Chalk it up to being a fellow American." He gave her a quick, probing look. "A very pretty one."

CANDLELIGHT SUPREMES

DANGER IN PARADISE

Kit Daley

A CANDLELIGHT SUPREME

Published by
Dell Publishing Co., Inc.
1 Dag Hammarskjold Plaza
New York, New York 10017

ISBN: 0-440-11714-3

Printed in the United States of America

January 1987

10 9 8 7 6 5 4 3 2 1

WFH

To Our Readers:

We are pleased and excited by your overwhelmingly positive response to our Candlelight Supremes. Unlike all the other series, the Supremes are filled with more passion, adventure, and intrigue, and are obviously the stories you like best.

In months to come we will continue to publish books by many of your favorite authors as well as the very finest work from new authors of romantic fiction. As always, we are striving to present unique, absorbing love stories —the very best love has to offer.

Breathtaking and unforgettable, Supremes follow in the great romantic tradition you've come to expect *only* from Candlelight Romances.

Your suggestions and comments are always welcome. Please let us hear from you.

Sincerely,

The Editors
Candlelight Romances
1 Dag Hammarskjold Plaza
New York, New York 10017

DANGER IN
PARADISE

CHAPTER ONE

As Samantha Prince leaned forward to straighten the books on a lower shelf, her long braid fell across her shoulder. Impatiently she flipped it back, considering again whether she should cut it short. Some people called her hair-color auburn; she called it red. Fiery-haired auburns were the heroines in the books she read; the color did not describe herself.

"Samantha, what do you think of this book? I'm going out of town again and need something to keep me warm at night," a stylish businesswoman in her forties said.

"A very good mystery, Mrs. Carson, but I wasn't impressed with the main character. Not enough backbone to get out of all the scrapes he and the heroine got into."

"It sounds like more adventure than mystery. Once I start a good adventure I can't put it down and end up reading through the night. All those cliff-hangers, you know." Mrs. Carson scanned another book from a display near the checkout counter.

Samantha smiled to herself. Mrs. Carson always came into her store right before a business trip and went through almost every book on the shelves, looking for just the right one that was a great story but wouldn't keep her up past midnight. Samantha had never found a novel with both ingredients, and she read at least half the books that came through her store. It was her favorite pastime, to lose herself in the lives of the characters and imagine herself doing things that she would never do in her real life.

"Maybe I should try a romance this time," Mrs. Carson continued, shifting her attention to another section. "The last mystery I read had me waking up every time I heard anything. And you know in a hotel how many sounds you can hear."

Actually, she didn't, Samantha reflected. She had never been anywhere, unless she counted visiting Aunt Lou. She had planned a trip to Europe two summers before but had to cancel it. She was beginning to believe her lack of travel experience was a crime at the age of thirty.

"A good love story," Samantha said, indicating the book Mrs. Carson picked up. "That ought to keep you warm at night. It's very hot."

She waved her hand to show just how hot the book was.

While Mrs. Carson examined both books again, Samantha glanced around at the rows of bookshelves. After three years her business was doing very well—at least well enough for her to afford a vacation. Maybe she'd go to some exotic place, she thought as Mrs. Carson decided to buy both the romance and the mystery.

When Mrs. Carson left the Purple Ink, the noise of New Orleans traffic and a blast of cold air rushed into the shop. Samantha shivered and pulled the front of her brown sweater more securely across her chest. Somewhere exotic and warm, she amended. In Samantha's mind the only good thing to come from cold weather was curling up in bed under layers of wool blankets with a great book to read while sipping a steaming cup of hot chocolate with lots of marshmallows in it.

Tonight, she vowed as she began to finish restocking the shelves of the adventure section. Pausing to examine a cover on one book, she was instantly reminded of her younger brother, Mark, who traveled the world, going from one adventure to the next while she remained in New Orleans, working day after day to make Purple Ink a success. The biggest adventure Samantha ever encountered was the rush hour traffic on Interstate 10.

11

Sighing heavily, she completed her task and noted it was time to close up for the day. Standing, she stretched to ease the ache in her lower back. It was time to start exercising again, Samantha thought. The holiday season had been busy and she got out of the routine once Thanksgiving had passed. Now it was the first of February, and she had ignored her better sense and found excuse after excuse not to get back to it. Though exercising would never head her list of favorite things to do, she vowed to sign up for a new aerobics class.

"Samantha, I'm going. I'll see you tomorrow morning at nine thirty," Nell, Samantha's assistant, said as she gathered up her purse and coat.

"Don't forget we have to start the inventory tomorrow. Can you stay late?"

"Yes."

"I have everything lined up, so it shouldn't take as long as last year."

Nell shook her head. "You are the most organized human being I've ever met. If I know you, you'll have devised a way to cut our time nearly in half."

"Oh, at least. Why else invest in a computer?" Samantha laughed and waved her friend on.

Nell was always teasing Samantha about how neat and orderly she was. But she had practically raised her younger brother while her mother had worked to support them. As a teenager she had juggled school, part-time work, and housework. It hadn't been easy, but her mother and younger brother had depended on her, so she had learned to be organized the hard way.

Samantha went through the same routine to close her shop as she had done ever since she had bought it. She flipped the closed sign on the door and locked it. Then she tallied the day's sales and took the extra money out of the register to deposit at the bank on her way home. After one final survey of her store, she went out the back door to her car.

Mark always laughed about her and her routines, but they gave her a sense of security and stability that was important to her. Neither she nor Mark, as children, nor their mother, had had much of either; it didn't seem to bother her brother, but it did bother her.

Because it was Thursday, after depositing the money in the bank Samantha stopped by the grocery store on her way home, then the gas station. She hated missing the nightly news on Thursday, but she liked to have her only day off, Sunday, free for whatever she wanted to do.

At the gas station Bert rubbed his hands up and down his arms and said, "I guarantee this winter has been the coldest in years! Every time that door opens I feel it down to me bones."

Bert's father, the owner of the station, came into the office. "Howdy, Samantha. The usual, ten dollars?"

"You got my number." She grinned at the father and son. She had traded at their gas station for years and could depend on them if anything went wrong with her car. It was a secure feeling because her car was now five years old and starting to act up.

When she finally arrived at her house it was late and she was tired. She picked up the bag of groceries and was planning her dinner as she stepped into her house. The phone was ringing, and she nearly dropped the bag as she rushed to pick up the receiver.

"Hello, Samantha Prince speaking."

"Sam! My God, you're home finally." Her brother's voice was faint, but he sounded frantic.

"Mark, what's wrong? Where in the world are you?" Samantha shifted her weight to set the grocery bag on the kitchen table.

"Manaus."

The long distance connection wasn't a good one and Samantha had to strain to hear his answer. "The Amazon?"

"Yes."

"The last I heard you were in Rio. Why are you there?" She had read plenty of books set in

14

the jungle and couldn't imagine anyone wanting to go there.

"It's a long story. I don't have the time to go into it."

The tone of her brother's voice, laced with impatience, alarmed Samantha. Tiny prickles of fear rose on the nape of her neck. "Why did you call?" She forced her voice to remain calm while her grip tightened on the receiver. He was her only close relative, their mother having died four years before. Though they didn't see each other a lot, she loved him very much and their relationship was a good one.

"I need a thousand dollars to get out of here. I needed it yesterday. Can you send me the money?" Mark's voice faded in and out.

"You said you need a thousand dollars?"

"Yes, Sis. Fast."

There was no mistaking the desperation in his answer. The tingles of fear quickly spread down her body. "Are you in some kind of trouble?" As a child she had rescued her brother from a few situations. He had always been daring; there was a bold recklessness about him that was very appealing, yet dangerous too. They were like night and day.

He laughed, but there was no amusement in the sound. "You could say that. I have someone who would like to get his hands on me. Can you wire it, Sis?"

"Yes, of course. But I can't do anything until tomorrow morning. Everything is closed."

"Damn! I'll try to make—wait for it."

"Where are you staying?"

"The Grand Hotel. It doesn't live up to its name, but it's all I could afford."

"Can I send it to you there?"

"No! I'll have to pick it up at the bank. It's safer. I can't trust anyone."

Samantha shuddered. "Safer? Mark, please tell me what's going on."

Static crackled over the line, and Samantha placed her hand over her other ear as if that would help her hear him better.

"If anything happens to me, Sam, there's something of great value under the altar of the Para Mission church. Got that?"

"Yes, but—"

There was the sound of male voices in the background, then Mark said quickly, "Got to go. Love you."

The phone went dead.

Samantha collapsed into a chair, her whole body trembling. She thought about pinching herself; surely she had dreamed the telephone conversation. But the fear and sense of urgency reminded her of the reality of the phone call, and she was chilled with dread.

Something of great value under the altar of the Para Mission church?

What? How was Mark involved? Was it illegal? Why was he running scared? And from whom? Her mind felt as if it would explode from all the unanswered questions bombarding her.

A thousand dollars! That would wipe out most of her savings for her vacation, but if Mark was in trouble, Samantha would sell her house and store if she had to.

If Mark was in trouble. From the sound of his voice he was in trouble. She knew she would be at the bank first thing in the morning.

Samantha stood frozen, holding her check for one thousand dollars in both hands. Mark hadn't picked it up. It was hard for her to believe that her money had been returned that morning. But if he was going to pick it up, Mark would have in a week's time.

Her hands began to shake and she almost dropped the check. What or who had prevented her brother from getting the money?

The questions she had been avoiding all morning invaded her thoughts, and she sank into her desk chair in the back of her store.

"What should I do?" she asked the silent walls.

Call! She'd call him at the Grand Hotel in Manaus. Maybe he was still there and didn't need the money anymore and that was why he hadn't picked it up. Maybe everything was fine now. Maybe the moon really was made of cheese.

Apprehensive about what she would find out, Samantha placed an international call to Brazil. When the man who answered at the hotel couldn't speak English, she was at a loss.

"May I speak with Señor Prince?" Samantha spoke very slowly and in a loud voice, as if that would make things clear. She had never been good at learning foreign languages and envied her brother, who knew five fluently.

The stream of words that followed was unintelligible. Frustrated, Samantha finally hung up, concluding there was no Señor Prince at the Grand Hotel. Next she put a call through to Mark's apartment in Rio and prayed that her brother would answer. On the twentieth ring she gave up and slammed the phone down, even more frustrated than before. Her fear returned in full force.

For five minutes she stared at the check, her mind churning with possible courses of action. Suddenly she snatched up the receiver and dialed again. Five minutes later she had booked a flight to Rio.

She would go to Mark's place in Rio and find out what she could find out about his whereabouts. Since he was no longer at the hotel in Manaus, maybe he had returned to Rio and wasn't in his apartment at the moment. She would keep calling until she had to leave the next morning, Samantha decided, and hope that she was panicking for no reason.

Thirty minutes later she was on her way home to pack for Brazil, having left a stunned Nell behind to run the bookstore. When she had thought about a vacation in a warm, exotic place last week, this wasn't how she had envisioned planning it. Samantha had imagined herself going to a travel agent and getting plenty of brochures on different tropical locales. Then she would have gone home, spread them all out on her kitchen table, and slowly read through each one until she had narrowed her selection down to one. Everything would have been done in an orderly, slow fashion. Wasn't part of the joy of a vacation the anticipation beforehand?

While sitting at a stoplight, her conversation with Nell returned to Samantha's mind.

"I can't believe you're dropping everything to go to Brazil to look for your brother! This isn't you. You don't do things like this," Nell had said.

"My brother doesn't disappear like this either. I can't sit here and wonder what's happened to him. I've got to find out. I can't get any answers over the phone."

"So you're flying thousands of miles to get some answers?"

"Do you know of a better way?"

Nell had shaken her head. "Don't worry

about the shop. I'll take care of it. If your brother calls, what should I tell him?"

"Find out where he is and tell him to stay put. I'll check in with you every few days."

Horns blared behind Samantha, and she realized she was sitting at a green light with angry motorists waiting on her. Embarrassed, she gunned her engine and sped forward.

She welcomed the familiarity of her small house, and before attempting to pack, she fixed herself a cup of hot tea and sat down at the kitchen table to organize what she had to do in the next twelve hours before she left for Rio.

Passport. Thank goodness she had one from that aborted trip to Europe.

Clothes? What kind of clothes should she take to Rio? Wasn't it summer there? Clothing for a hot, humid environment. A couple of sundresses. Maybe a pair or two of shorts. A bathing suit. Sandals.

The last thing Samantha put on her list of necessities was the latest book she was reading, *Jungle Fever*. It was part of a shipment that had arrived at the store the previous day. Samantha had been drawn to the title because of Mark, but now she could hardly put it down. It was an engrossing tale of adventure and intrigue by a new author whom Samantha thought would go far. She had gotten to the part where the hero had just rescued the heroine from a tribe of headhunters and they were fleeing for their lives.

With her list completed she began to pack and finished at eleven. After showering and getting ready for bed, she tried to sleep, but her mind danced with images of her brother, herself, and his unknown enemy. She sat up in bed, switched on the light, and started reading the next chapter of her book.

Harper swung the machete, striking the thick undergrowth over and over. The swish of the blade filled the jungle stillness with the urgency of their escape. Diana clung to Harper's hand, glancing constantly over her shoulders as they raced through the jungle. She could hear the Indians behind her. She could imagine their savage faces as the headhunters followed, so sure she and Harper would be caught. This was the headhunters' territory. They ruled it as they had for hundreds of years: by fear.

Samantha was immediately whisked into another world and didn't put the novel down until she couldn't keep her eyelids open another minute. She glanced at her bedside clock and gasped. It was three in the morning. She had to leave at seven!

Sleep finally descended, but it was a restless sleep, saturated with pictures of painted Indians with lip discs and spears tipped in poison. Samantha tossed and turned, visualizing herself as Diana as she last read about her: standing at the top of a waterfall with a rushing river in front of her and the headhunters in back. Either way Diana went appeared to be instant death.

Cold reality returned the next morning as Samantha rushed to make her flight to Rio via Miami. She wasn't able to catch her breath until the plane was in the air and the meal was being served.

Then the idea of what she was doing struck her with a powerful impact. She was flying down to Rio with one day's notice, trying to locate her brother in one of the largest countries in the world. She wasn't a detective and really knew nothing, other than what she had read, about what a detective did to find a missing person.

What was happening to the sensible, logical woman she was?

That question returned to plague her in Rio as she waited while her brother's neighbor, whom Mark had said always had his spare key, let her into Mark's place. Before her lay the wreckage of a once presentable bachelor's apartment. Everything was torn or shattered, nothing left untouched. Someone had searched this place very thoroughly, and she knew it was connected with Mark's mysterious phone call the week before.

Samantha moved slowly into her brother's

apartment. Suddenly she knew the fear Diana felt looking down at the rushing river. And Samantha knew what she had to do next: go to the Amazon.

CHAPTER TWO

Brock Slader watched the dark Latin man sitting across the table. He had dreaded this meeting, and now Brock paused to sip his thick Brazilian coffee and try to gain some control of himself, of the situation. The conversation was not going the way he had hoped.

Brock welcomed the stirring of the air from the overhead fan as his gray eyes met the man's black ones. Each appraised the other; Brock concluded that the Latin meant every word of his threat.

Brock set his cup down and stared into the man's dark eyes. "Okay," he replied, "I'll do it. It seems I don't have any other choice."

"No, my friend, you don't." The Latin stood, shook his hand, and left.

Disgusted, Brock tossed a few bills onto the table and started for the lobby of the hotel where he had to wait. He found a lumpy chair that had a clear view of the front door and sat down.

* * *

Samantha entered the lobby of the Grand Hotel and instantly understood why Mark had said the hotel didn't live up to its name. The furniture with its faded material and scratched wood had seen better days. The tiles were worn and several ceiling fans were the only means of cooling the room. The humidity of the jungle city at the "wedding" of two mighty rivers, the Amazon and the Rio Negro, was stifling.

But at the moment Samantha didn't care about those things. She only wanted to locate her brother, and this was the last place he had been heard from. Mark hadn't returned to Rio as she had hoped; no one there had seen him in weeks.

She squared her shoulders and walked up to the reception desk, setting her suitcase on the floor beside her, then rummaging through her purse until she found the pamphlet she had been looking for. *Spanish for the Traveler* was the only thing she had had in her store, and though she had known Spanish wasn't the official language of Brazil, she had grabbed it as she had left her store.

She flipped through the pamphlet until she came to the phrase she wanted, praying her high school Spanish would be enough in a country that spoke Portuguese. Why hadn't she stocked up on some phrase books in Portuguese?

"Do you speak English?" Samantha winced at her awful imitation of Spanish; she had barely made passing grades in the subject in high school.

The young man behind the desk frowned and looked at her questioningly.

"Uhh . . ." Samantha scanned her phrase book. Weren't the Portuguese and Spanish languages alike, at least enough for her to be understood? She tried again in her stilted Spanish, "Do you speak Spanish?"

The clerk began to speak rapidly, but not in Spanish or English. Samantha didn't understand a word he said. Why did Brazil have to be the only country in South America that didn't speak Spanish? she wondered desperately. Then she would have at least had a fighting chance—well, maybe a fighting chance to be understood.

Samantha held up her hand to stop his flow of words, but it seemed he didn't even understand sign language. She glanced about frantically and her gaze collided with a man's across the lobby. Amusement brightened his gray eyes, and he rose to his feet and strode toward her in one fluid motion.

"May I help?" he asked in flawless English with a slight Texan drawl.

"You're American!" Relief transformed her frown into a wide smile of gratitude.

"I couldn't help overhearing your little exchange with this gentleman. Trouble, ma'am?"

His silver-bright eyes took an inventory of her features and left a heated trail where they roamed. He catalogued and assessed, all in a minute's time.

Samantha blushed. She waved her clutch purse in front of her face as if she were flushed because of the heat, not the stranger before her. She knew she should say something in reply to his question, but she kept wondering what the result of his appraisal was. She couldn't tell by his closed look.

One of his dark eyebrows rose. "Ma'am?"

This heat must be affecting her brain; she couldn't seem to form a simple answer as she returned his bold survey, cataloguing *his* features as roughly hewn and bronze, assessing *his* appearance as rugged and earthy.

The clerk behind the desk said something to the man, drawing his intense gaze from her and breaking his hypnotic hold. He answered in what Samantha supposed was Portuguese.

She clutched her purse to her chest and finally said, "I don't speak Portuguese and I'm trying to find my brother, who was staying here."

The stranger's gaze shifted back to her, and she felt warm again. His look was penetratingly disconcerting, as though it could cut right through to the heart of a person. "What's your brother's name?"

"Mark Prince."

"I'll see what I can find out"—his gaze swerved to her left hand—"Miss Prince."

For the next few minutes Samantha tried to follow the conversation but found her mind instead drawn to the man questioning the young clerk. His voice was deep and rich with a slightly husky timbre. He had broad shoulders and a muscular torso that tapered down to a narrow waist and slim hips. He was tall, with a self-confidence that Samantha didn't see in many people. It was conveyed in how he walked, talked, carried himself.

"I'm sorry, but your brother isn't here."

She was so absorbed in her study of the man that it took a few seconds for Samantha to realize he was talking to her in English. She blinked, wishing she had been listening to what he had said, not how he had said it.

"Your brother isn't here," he repeated.

By the sparkling gleam in the stranger's eye Samantha could tell he knew why she hadn't been paying attention, and it had had nothing to do with her concern for her brother's welfare. "He was staying here last week. When did he check out?" She really wasn't surprised that her brother wasn't there. She had come to the

28

hotel because it was a starting point for her in her search.

More words were exchanged between the men before he turned to her and said, "He didn't check out."

"I thought you said Mark isn't here."

He smiled, a slow uplifting of the corners of his mouth that could only be described as sexy. "He isn't. It seems your brother skipped out on paying his bill a week ago."

Shock stole her next words. But her shock quickly receded to be replaced by the fear that she had been fighting to control ever since her brother had called. Mark would never do that. Unless . . .

"Did he take his things with him?" Samantha asked, feeling as though the expansive lobby were rapidly moving in on her.

"No, this man put them in a back storeroom."

"Please ask him if I may have them."

The stranger spoke to the man, then said to Samantha, "For the price of your brother's hotel bill."

"How much?" Samantha asked warily.

When he mentioned a ridiculously high amount, she exclaimed, "For this place?"

"I think he's throwing in some for his trouble. It really isn't all that much in American dollars. It just sounds like a lot in Brazilian currency."

"Very well." Samantha withdrew her wallet and counted out the money, practically slamming it down on the counter. She was frustrated, confused, tired, hot, and getting absolutely nowhere.

"Anything else, Miss Prince?"

She looked up at the man. "Yes. Would you please see if he has a room available for me?"

"Here?"

She nodded.

"Are you sure? There are better places to stay than at the Grand Hotel, especially for"—his gaze traveled down the length of her then back up to her face—"for a woman alone."

"Are you staying here?" Her question came out in a breathless rush; she had never felt so possessed by a look.

"Yes, but I'm—"

"A man," she said dryly, ready to defend her female status.

He chuckled. "I am a man. I can't deny that."

And neither could Samantha as she matched the challenge in his eyes with one of her own. His regard held an intensity that she had seldom encountered, and yet it was strangely unfathomable.

"But that wasn't what I was going to say, Miss Prince. I'm familiar with the language and you aren't. No one here speaks English."

"Or Spanish," Samantha said wryly.

"You should stay at one of the bigger hotels."

"I can't. My brother might return for his things."

"Not if he skipped out."

"But he didn't! Something's wrong. Mark isn't like that."

"When was the last time you saw your brother?"

"Two years ago."

"A lot can happen to a person in two years." He said it as though he knew from experience.

She lifted her chin, her eyes narrowing slightly. "I'm staying. It would be easier if you asked the clerk—please."

The man shrugged and made the arrangements for a room for Samantha. The young clerk insisted that she pay for two nights in advance and again she dug into her wallet and paid the man his price. So this was what it was like to travel and stay in a hotel, Samantha thought. Mrs. Carson could have it.

After signing her name to the register, the clerk escorted Samantha and the stranger to the storeroom to retrieve her brother's one suitcase.

Back in the lobby Samantha turned to the man and said, "I'm Samantha Prince. I'd like to treat you to lunch for helping me."

He shook his head. "You don't have to."

"Please. If you hadn't come to my rescue, I'd

31

still be trying to figure out what the man was saying, Mr. . . ."

"Brock Slader." He glanced about the lobby, indecision in his eyes. Then suddenly, as though he had made up his mind, he looked down at her and replied, "Fine. I'll meet you here in an hour then."

As Samantha started to pick up the two pieces of luggage, Brock intercepted her and took them instead. Their hands touched and a bolt of electricity streaked up her arm. She snatched away her hand.

In answer to the question in her eyes he said, "There are no elevators in this hotel. The third floor is a long way up."

As they climbed the first flight of stairs, Samantha said, "I'm in your debt again. After all the traveling I've done in the last forty-eight hours, I don't think I'd have made it up this first flight with the luggage."

"It's nothing."

Samantha had to agree that the two bags appeared to give him no trouble at all. He apparently was a man who prided himself in keeping in shape, a man capable of taking care of himself if he got into trouble. She instantly thought of Harper in *Jungle Fever.*

At her door he placed the suitcases on the floor. "Maybe it would be better if you got some rest this afternoon. The jungle has a way of sapping a person's strength—male or female."

His half grin sent her heart beating at a fast pace. "I have to eat. I'll rest tonight."

Tilting his head forward in a slight nod, he drawled, "Very well."

Samantha couldn't resist the temptation of watching him saunter away. She was again reminded of Harper's quick reflexes and animal grace. When Brock was at the end of the hallway, he glanced back and touched an imaginary Stetson in salute. Samantha winced at her blatant behavior and immediately turned her attention to inserting her key in the lock.

When she was inside her room, she swung Mark's suitcase up on the bed and tried to open it. It was locked. She took out a metal fingernail file and tried to pick the lock, but that didn't work and she decided to give it up for the moment. She hid the bag under her bed, then sat down.

For the first time she took a moment to examine her surroundings. It was a small room that had an old bed with no headboard and a faded bedspread, a table with a water stain in the middle of it, and one chest with several long drawers. At least, Samantha thought, the room seemed clean, and there was even a small balcony that overlooked the street.

Suddenly Samantha experienced an overwhelming feeling of loneliness. She wanted to

33

be home, back in the safe world of her store and house. Even the New Orleans traffic would be a welcome sight at the moment—it was familiar, something she could handle. She wasn't at all sure she could handle this place, this situation.

She was used to being independent, and already she was depending on a stranger—a very appealing man, but a stranger nonetheless. Well, the sooner she found her brother, the sooner she could return to New Orleans and the security there.

Samantha pushed herself off the bed and headed for the tiny bathroom. After splashing some water on her face and neck, she felt a little better. She changed into a fresh sundress, pale yellow cotton with thin straps and a soft flowing skirt. She left her hair in its long braid and twisted it on top of her head. Even that was cooler in this heat. And just a week ago she had wanted to vacation in a warm, exotic place. This city was certainly warm, but she couldn't say it was exotic.

As she left the room to meet Brock Slader in the lobby, she mentally listed the things she had to do that afternoon. First she would go to the bank where the money had been cabled to Mark. Then, if she had to, she'd go to the police. And lastly, she would visit as many hotels in the area as possible.

Going over her list, Samantha knew it wasn't

going to be easy if the bank and police couldn't help her. But maybe Mark had checked out of the Grand Hotel and was staying somewhere else in Manaus. She had to exhaust all possibilities before ...

She shook her head to rid her mind of any unpleasant thoughts. Mark was okay, she assured herself. He was like a cat, always landing on his feet. And like a cat, Mark seemed to have nine lives.

When she entered the lobby she spied Brock, reclining against a white pillar, his arms and legs loosely crossed as he watched people entering and leaving the hotel. His stance looked casual, but for some reason Samantha felt there wasn't anything casual about him.

Even in white pants and shirt she could tell his body was muscular and well-conditioned. If it weren't for his gray eyes, a startling combination against his dark features, he could easily have been mistaken for a Latin because of his tanned skin and black hair.

Samantha realized she only knew his name. Beyond that, all she knew was that he spoke fluent Portuguese. Usually she was very cautious, especially where men were concerned, but she had no one else to turn to. She knew no one in this country and she realized she needed help if she was going to find her brother.

He looked her way; their gazes caught and

held. Brock unfolded his arms and legs and eased away from the pillar. Striding toward her, he kept his eyes fastened to hers. She felt the heat of his probing gaze, and suddenly she wondered if she were plunging into something that was way out of her league.

When they were a few feet apart, Brock's gaze swept down her body, pausing for the briefest moment at her small waist. If any other man had looked at her so thoroughly, she would have instantly been on guard. But ever since this journey began, nothing had been the same. Samantha felt like a different person, which at times was even more confusing than her brother's disappearance.

"You can do a lot in an hour's time," Brock said in his southwestern drawl.

"I feel like a new woman," Samantha replied, meaning it on more than one level.

"We don't want to eat here. I know a little restaurant a few blocks away that has good food and reasonable prices."

"That sounds like my kind of place."

Brock touched her elbow to lead the way and once again she felt tingles streaking up her arm. Her instant physical response to him was unnerving. Would it always be like this, the slightest touch triggering off a chain reaction in her body?

Samantha no longer had to wonder if she were plunging into something out of her league; she felt it deep within her, and knew she would do nothing to stop this exciting journey into the unknown.

At the restaurant Brock asked for a table in the corner that afforded them a view of the rest of the room. After assisting her into a chair, he sat with his back to the wall next to her, much too close for Samantha's peace of mind.

Samantha allowed him to order for her, since she couldn't read the menu. Besides, she didn't think she would eat a bite when the food did arrive. Her stomach was twisted into a huge knot. She told herself it was because of her brother, but in her heart she knew this man next to her was the real cause.

After the waitress left, Brock reclined in his chair and studied Samantha a moment under lowered lashes. "You're here because your brother is missing?"

"Yes." Her throat was so dry that her answer came out in a whisper.

"For how long?"

"A week."

"Lady, that isn't long in this town. People often disappear into the jungle for much longer."

His piercing gray eyes seemed to penetrate, trying to read her mind. She looked away and wished the waitress would return with her drink. "There's more to it than just that."

"What?"

37

She looked back at him and wondered how much she should tell this man. She needed someone to help her; she couldn't find Mark alone. Was Brock Slader that someone?

His piercing eyes gentled. "Maybe talking about it will help."

She drew in a deep breath and said, "Mark called me last week. He said he was in trouble and needed money to get out of here. I wired him the money but he never picked it up." Her voice caught and she swallowed several times. "Someone was after him and I'm afraid . . ."

He leaned forward, covering her small hand with his large one. "Maybe he's in hiding. There are a lot of places a person can get lost around here."

"I'm praying that's it, but I have to know. He's my only family."

His hand tightened about hers, and they both glanced down at their clasped hands as if they finally realized they were touching. Brock slowly withdrew his hand and sat back in his chair.

"Why is your brother in trouble? Who's after him?"

"I don't know, which makes it even worse. He didn't have time to tell me." Or he didn't want to tell her.

After the waitress brought their lunches, a baked pirarucu dish, Brock asked, "How are

38

you going to try to locate your brother? You're at a disadvantage, you know."

Disadvantage was putting it mildly. She was at a loss. But she had to try. "I realize I don't speak the language and I'm unfamiliar with this city, but—"

"That's not all," he said before she could finish. "This city is on the fringe of the jungle, a hostile, primitive environment that isn't too kind to people, especially novices—whether they're male or female, by the way. The jungle doesn't make a distinction between the sexes. You have no business being here. If your brother can't take care of himself, then how do you expect to take care of him?"

She stared down at her plate, knowing everything he said was true. When her gaze touched his again, she whispered, "With your help?"

Surprise flickered into his eyes. "My help! You don't even know me, lady."

"I don't know anyone here."

"My job isn't to rescue damsels in distress. I can't help you."

Gripping her fork and knife in her hands, Samantha leaned toward him, her expression intense. "I'm not in distress. It's my brother who needs help."

"Are you ready to do battle with those?" Brock's amused gaze flicked to the utensils in her hands then back to her face.

She glanced down and laughed. "No. I was about to try the fish and got caught up in the moment."

He smiled, first with his eyes and then his mouth. "Are you always this fervent?"

"No." But that was another aspect of her that seemed to be changing.

"Just about your brother. You must love him a lot."

"Do you have any family, Mr. Slader?"

"A father and a sister."

"Then maybe you can understand how important this is to me."

"I'm not a guide, and I'm certainly no detective." He frowned.

"I just need someone who knows the language and the city for a few days. I'll pay you for your services."

He didn't say anything.

"Do you have something better to do? Fifty dollars a day."

"I'm free for the rest of the day. But beyond that I can't guarantee my services."

"What are you doing in Manaus?"

"It's not important." He began to eat, dismissing the subject. "This is good. You'll need your energy if we're going to walk the streets, so to speak."

She watched him eat for a few minutes and realized that by not answering her he had intrigued her even more. Why was he in the Amazon? Why was it a secret?

"Lesson number one, Miss Prince: You'll need every ounce of strength you can get in the Amazon. Dieting has no place in the jungle."

She started to eat, forcing down half the delicious fish before she gave up and just finished her fruit drink. When she was nervous, she could never eat.

After he was through eating, Brock sipped his thick, sweet coffee and asked, "Where does your search begin?"

"At the bank where I wired the money, then the police."

"The bank is a waste of time. If he didn't pick it up, he didn't pick it up. We'll go to the police first." He handed her the check.

For a few seconds she stared at the bill, then at him. She was so used to the men she knew and dated paying the bill that it took a moment for her to realize she was to pay. But then, this certainly wasn't a date—and Brock Slader was nothing like the men she was used to seeing!

"This was your treat?" His dark eyebrows rose.

She took the tab and laid the money to cover it on the table.

Once outside the restaurant, Brock halted her progress with a hand on her arm. He turned her to face him. "Before we go to the police, are you prepared for the worst?"

41

CHAPTER THREE

"Don't worry. You won't have an hysterical woman on your hands. I don't go in for that." Samantha's voice held none of the confidence she wanted. She told herself that it was the humidity and strangeness of the jungle city. But in truth all her senses converged on the touch of Brock's hand on her arm, his fingers a tantalizing combination of rough and gentle.

Brock released his hold on her but didn't move away. He was only inches from her, his male scent mingling with the potent odors of the tropics carried on the moisture-laden breeze. The noise of Manaus surrounded them, but all Samantha could hear was the loud pounding of her heart that filled her ears.

"I knew a man who disappeared about six months back without a trace. There are a lot of stories like that, Miss Prince."

"I'm sure there are, but I'll find Mark. I would know if something had happened to him."

The warm gleam in his eyes that made them appear almost silver was gone, replaced by a serious look that turned his gaze a dark gray like storm clouds. "It will be worse if you discover nothing."

"Worse?"

"The jungle has a way of swallowing people up. You may never find out what's happened to your brother. You may spend the rest of your life hoping for something that won't happen."

Her eyes widened. "What has made you so cynical?"

"Reality," he replied tersely, his expression suddenly very closed. His stance forbade further discussion of the subject.

Samantha took a step back, trying to distance herself from his very masculine presence. "Are you saying I should hope to find my brother dead rather than not at all?" she asked incredulously.

Brock's mouth thinned; his eyes narrowed. Damnation! Looking at Samantha Prince at that moment stirred something in him he didn't need or want—a protective instinct. Wisps of her fiery hair had escaped her bun and framed her face. Not a beautiful face by most people's standards but definitely intriguing, he decided as his gaze took in the angry tilt of her head, the glint in her sherry-colored eyes, the frown on her full lips, the sprinkle of freckles on her upturned nose.

"For your information, Mr. Slader, I'll take the unknown over that kind of certainty any day."

She stormed past him without the slightest idea where she was going. Brock Slader had none of the characteristics of the rescuer of her dreams. Well, maybe a few of the physical traits, she amended reluctantly, scanning the side street she had absently turned down and finally realizing that she was totally lost.

The street was narrow, and she couldn't see very well because the buildings created deep shadows. She was already halfway down it, so she hurried toward the opening at the other end, her gaze skipping from one dark doorway to another. She had to fight the urge to run. Her vivid imagination conjured up men lurking in the shadows, ready to spring out as she walked by.

Hugging her purse close, as though it were her shield of armor, Samantha fixed her gaze on the cars passing through the intersection ahead and continued walking.

A hand grabbed her arm and she froze. She wished now more than ever that she had taken a self-defense class. She yanked away from the grasp and was suddenly freed. She stumbled forward and was caught again—this time by two muscular arms winding about her waist.

Samantha didn't have to look at the face of her "assailant" to know it was Brock Slader. His scent engulfed her, creating a tingling reaction that she desperately wanted to ignore. But that proved impossible. The feel of his chest against her back sent her pulse racing. Damn her traitorous body! It certainly wasn't going along with her level-headed side.

"The police station is this way." Brock steadied her, his arms still loosely about her as he nodded his head to indicate the direction she had come from.

She gazed up into his face, too close for her peace of mind, and saw the mischievous sparkle dance to life in his eyes. He was certainly enjoying himself!

Pulling herself from his embrace, she straightened her sundress with as much dignity as possible and put several feet between them, her chest rising and falling rapidly. "If you'll just give me directions, I'm sure I can find it on my own," she said in a haughty tone that didn't seem to dent his amused arrogance one bit.

"Most likely you'd become another lost soul in this jungle. I don't want to be responsible for that."

"I'm not your responsibility." She lifted her chin a fraction. She was determined to assert her independence; she had come alone to Brazil to find her brother and she would find him —*alone.*

He grinned, a flash of silver in his eyes.

"Even a cynic is allowed to have a heart every year or so. I guess you caught me when I was due." He shrugged, his expression innocent.

"Oh, how lucky for me." She walked past him back up the dimly lit side street, secretly glad he was beside her; but she would never tell him that. She didn't like depending on anyone, especially a stranger, but her common sense had always been strong, and right now it was telling her she needed help to find Mark.

They traversed the streets of Manaus in silence, Brock's steps quick and sure. Samantha was having a hard time keeping up with his pace, but she wasn't going to say a word to him. He would probably just comment on how out of shape she was—which she was painfully finding out to be true.

Her mind reeled from the heat and lack of sleep and food. She should have listened to Brock Slader earlier and at least eaten more. He would love for her to acknowledge that!

Lightheaded, Samantha stopped, placed a hand on her forehead, and drew in a shallow breath, then another, to calm her fast heartbeat. Brock glanced back at her.

Begrudgingly she murmured, "I have to rest for a few minutes."

He was instantly beside her, taking her elbow in his hand and guiding her toward some steps to sit down. "I forgot you're not used to this heat."

It was even worse when he was charming and gentlemanly, she thought; it did nothing to slow her heartbeat. And when he sat down beside her, his thigh touching hers on the narrow stairs, she decided the jungle air did strange things to people's heads and bodies.

She scooted over as far as possible on the two-foot-wide step and said lightly, "If I had known I was going to be doing this, I would never have given up my aerobics class." She waved her hand in front of her face, which did little to stir the stifling air, and exerted more energy than it was worth.

He didn't say anything. Instead, he leaned forward with his elbows resting on his lean, muscular thighs. His gaze was intent upon a spot near his foot.

Samantha reclined back and braced her arms on the step behind her. She studied Brock Slader, the afternoon sunlight illuminating his rich ebony hair, sprinkled with a few strands of silver. She sensed this man was tough, aggressive, individualistic, a man who shaped his own destiny. She wasn't sure where the impression came from, but it was strong like the slope of his jawline, the feel of his hand on her, the sharp look in his silver-gray eyes that delved inside a person to discern the hidden meaning behind words spoken. She knew he could move quickly and silently to take a person by surprise as he had with her on the side street.

Questions inundated her. Why was he in the Amazon? What did he do for a living? Why had he come after her?

Samantha voiced one of the many questions she wanted answered. "Why did you say it would be better if I knew my brother was dead than not discover anything?"

"Not better, just easier on you emotionally in the long run." He propped his chin on his loosely laced hands and continued to stare at the spot near his feet.

She couldn't see his face, but in his voice she heard concern, and something else she couldn't quite figure out. "I don't see how it could be easier on me emotionally. Mark and I are very close. He's all I have. There were times I felt more like a mother to him than a big sister."

He looked at her and for a brief moment Samantha saw anguish in his gaze. Then his expression became shuttered. His gray eyes, deep and intense, evaluated her much as she had assessed him only a few minutes before. There was an almost physical element to his gaze, and she felt as if she had opened up a painful chapter in his life.

"Believe me. I've seen what uncertainty can do to a person." Brock rolled to his feet and offered his hand to help her up. "We'd better get moving. We have a lot of ground to cover."

Samantha fitted her hand in his and rose.

"How much farther to the police station?" she asked in order to put their conversation on a less personal level. Suddenly she wasn't sure she could handle anything more.

"Only two more blocks."

She fell into step beside him, and this time he slowed his pace for her. When they arrived at the station, she allowed Brock to ask the questions, since the man in charge couldn't speak English. She had to acknowledge again how indebted she was to Brock after just a few short hours.

When he was satisfied with the answers the policeman gave him, he turned to Samantha and said, "Mark hasn't been found dead and he's not in jail. And there have been no unidentified bodies found in the last week."

She sighed with relief. "Thank goodness. Do you think we should check the hospitals?"

"I can call them when we return to the hotel, if you like."

"Yes. He could be hurt. I have to rule out every possibility."

"Do you want to report him missing?"

"Yes."

For the next thirty minutes Samantha, with Brock as her interpreter, answered questions concerning her brother. By the time they left the police station, she was exhausted.

Brock regarded her pale features and said, "I

think you should go back to the Grand Hotel and get some sleep."

Determined to cover as much ground as possible that day, she shook her head. "Let's visit a few hotels in the area first. Then I'll call it a day."

She wasn't sure she could solicit his help the next day, and at the police station she realized she needed someone who knew the language and the country. Brock was all she had at the moment, and if she had to, she would swallow her pride and ask him again for his help. Her brother's life might be at stake.

He hesitated.

"Please, Mr. Slader."

Her lovely brown eyes pleaded with him, and Brock found he couldn't say no, even though his common sense told him it was dangerous to become involved with Samantha Prince and her quest. He needed to keep his distance. She reminded him of all the things he had left behind in the States: security, normality, order.

"Okay, but when you find it's time to call it quits, tell me."

In one hotel all Brock got was glares. It was obvious a person didn't ask questions there. In another Samantha was relieved that Brock was with her. Several pairs of dark, lust-filled eyes examined every inch of her. How had she ever thought she could do this alone? For once she had done something without thinking and was now regretting her rash decision. And yet, she wouldn't have done anything differently. She couldn't have stayed in New Orleans just waiting to hear from her brother—or the authorities.

Ten hotels later Samantha said, "Uncle."

Brock looked over his shoulder at her and arched one thick brow.

"Quitting time."

His mouth quirked in a small grin. "Lady, I have to hand it to you. I thought you would quit four hotels back, especially when that drunk pinched you."

"You knew about that?"

Brock lounged against the side of a building, rubbing the back of his neck. "Ma'am, do you want me to go back and beat the living daylights out of him? By this time I'm sure he's passed out somewhere."

"What! No duel?" she asked mockingly.

"But I'm sure I can rouse him for a few punches."

"Well, no. I . . ." Exasperated at the smug look on Brock Slader's face, Samantha started down the street at a brisk pace that almost immediately slowed. Her legs were trembling from exhaustion.

"Miss Prince?"

She stopped and spun about.

"The hotel is this way."

Samantha walked back to him with all the dignity she could muster. Why did she have to have such a lousy sense of direction? Well, one thing was certain: she would never be an explorer or a seasoned traveler. She would constantly have to be rescued from getting lost.

The silent laughter in his gray eyes made her bristle. "Remind me to pick up a map of Manaus."

"I doubt that would help. You're right, you know. You do need a personal guide. If you don't mind me saying, I've never seen a person so ill equipped to search for another person. Before this is over your brother is going to have to look for you."

"I do mind you saying." Samantha stiffened her spine and began to head in the right direction.

His robust laughter drifted to her, and she gritted her teeth to keep her angry retort to herself. He had an uncanny ability to top each of her ripostes with one of his own, and it was getting on her nerves. She must be his afternoon entertainment. If she didn't need someone like him so much, she would tell him to get lost. But somehow she sensed he knew where he was at all times.

What was she going to do the next day? As exasperating as he was, Brock Slader was her only hope. She had to convince him to help her at least tomorrow. Her choices were limited, and right now he was her best option.

At the hotel Samantha stood beneath a fan and reluctantly asked, "Will you make the calls to the hospitals for me? I would except for one small detail. I don't speak the language." She attempted a smile and tried to look grateful.

He chuckled, a sound full of a husky presumption. "You don't have to turn those big brown eyes on me. I told you I would, and I will. But first don't you think we should have something to eat?"

"Are you asking me?"

The crinkles at the corners of his eyes deepened. "Yes, and I'm paying. The restaurant across the street is good."

"I must warn you: I'm no longer nervous and I'm famished."

"Maybe I should make you nervous." He took a step toward her, his eyes gleaming. "After all, my financial resources aren't unlimited."

She backed up until she collided with a pillar. He laid a hand at the side of her head, his mouth inches from hers. Running her tongue over her dry lips, Samantha turned wide eyes up toward his. Suddenly the teasing sparkle in his gaze vanished, and in its place there was a smoldering need. His mouth was a breath away. Every nerve ending vibrated with his nearness.

He straightened abruptly. "If I'm going to make those calls tonight, we'd better eat now. This has been a long day for both of us."

She had wanted him to kiss her! Her hand came up to cover a hot cheek. He was practically a stranger and her thoughts had raced with pictures of them embracing, kissing . . .

Again Samantha cursed her vivid imagination; it would cause her definite trouble one of these days. Pushing herself away from the pillar, she hoped her expression didn't give her thoughts away. Maybe he'd think her cheeks were flushed because of the heat. And maybe it would snow in Manaus.

Seated in the restaurant, Brock seemed content to let the silence lengthen between them. Silence made Samantha nervous and she sought to fill it.

"What do you do for a living, Mr. Slader?"

"Brock. Formalities are for the civilized world thousands of miles away."

Samantha waited for him to answer her question, but he lapsed back into his silence. "Yes, well, Brock, why are you in the Amazon?" she asked, using a different approach to discover more about him.

"Looking around." He sipped his drink and watched her over the rim of his glass.

"For what?"

"Something to make me money."

54

"Oh" was all Samantha could think of to say. They lapsed back into silence.

After their meals were served, Samantha tried to think of a way to ask him for his help again. This time she ate her fish with relish while mentally discarding one plea for help after another.

She had to appeal to his chivalrous side. No, he didn't have one.

Well, then, she could appeal to his greedy side. Yes, that he had.

"I'm glad to see you've got your appetite back. That must mean you're not nervous anymore."

"No, it only means my stomach overruled my nerves," she replied flippantly.

"I'm glad one part of you has common sense, Sam."

"Don't call me that!" Only Mark called her that. When her brother said Sam, it was a teasing name because she had been a tomboy while growing up. But when Brock said Sam, it made their relationship suddenly intimate, familiar.

"Why not?"

She grasped for a reason to put their relationship on a more formal level. "Because . . . because Mark does."

"Sam fits you better than Samantha."

She pressed her lips together and refused to say another word on the subject. If he wanted to call her Sam, she realized he would. She was beginning to see that Brock Slader lived by his own rules. Did the jungle do that to a person? Its harsh, unfamiliar environment certainly demanded a lot.

She waited until they were both through with their dinners before bringing up the subject of his help. She watched as he finished his after-dinner coffee. Now that she had decided what she would offer, how should she broach the subject? Finally she settled on the direct approach.

"You say you're in the Amazon for money. Well, I'm offering you a way to make some. All I need is a few days of your time. As I told you earlier, I'll pay you well for your assistance. In fact, I'll double my offer. One hundred dollars a day. And if we find Mark, I'll throw in a bonus." She paused to let her suggestion sink in. "From what I can gather, you need the money."

"No." Not one emotion flickered across his face.

"Do you have anything better to do for the next few days?" she asked skeptically.

"The answer is still no." He pulled out some money and tossed it on the table. "I'll take you back to your room, then make the calls from the lobby. If I have any news for you, I'll contact you." He rose, towering over her.

"Won't you at least think over my offer?

Please." She hated to resort to begging, but he had forced her to. She was desperate to find her brother.

"We'll meet tomorrow morning about the phone calls."

"Then that means you'll think over what I'm offering. Even in the States that's good money for a day's work."

"No, Sam. I merely meant we'll have breakfast together and I'll give you the rundown on the hospitals, so you'll know where you stand. Of course, if I find your brother in one, I'll let you know immediately."

"I'll wait with you in the lobby while you make the calls."

He gave her an intense stare. "No. I doubt I'll find out anything, since you would have heard through normal channels. But you look exhausted. There's no reason for both of us to stay up."

She was tired and didn't savor waiting in the Grand Hotel lobby, not after her experience in other hotel lobbies that day. Her room would serve the same purpose. "You promise you'll let me know right away if there's any chance he's at one of the hospitals?"

"Of course. Then you're on your own, Sam." He added the last as a reminder to himself to keep away from women like Samantha Prince.

Samantha had never felt so deflated in her life, but if he thought she had given up, he had a surprise in store for him the next morning at breakfast. Somehow she would come up with a way to convince him to help her, because as they had searched for her brother that afternoon, she had reluctantly realized that Brock had given her a sense of security. He was a man very capable of taking care of himself—and her. And some of the rough places she knew she would have to go to in her search called for a man like Brock.

As they walked back to the hotel, Samantha asked, "Have you traveled in the jungle much?"

"A bit."

"Do you know anything about the Para Mission?"

"I've never been there, but I know where it is. Why?"

"My brother mentioned it, that's all." She lifted her shoulders in a shrug, trying to appear casual.

Again Brock fell silent, and she realized how comfortable he was with silence. She supposed when a person traveled in the jungle he had to be comfortable with isolation. She loved people. That was what she liked most about her job, the customers who came into her store, the gossip, the small talk they exchanged.

As they mounted the third set of stairs at the Grand Hotel, Samantha felt her exhaustion

58

deep in her bones. She knew she'd never take an elevator for granted again.

At her door she turned toward Brock to set a time for their meeting the next morning. She was startled by his nearness, but with her back flattened against the door, she couldn't take a step away.

"What time?" she asked breathlessly.

"Tomorrow morning?"

She nodded, her throat tight.

"Eight."

"Fine. I'll . . ." Her voice faded as his hand reached up to cup her face.

His fingers slid around to the nape of her neck, and she thought her legs would buckle. When he started undoing her bun, her eyes grew round.

His eyes darkened and his voice was husky as he said, "I've been curious all day what your hair looks like down."

He combed his fingers through the mass of flaming curls and arranged it about her shoulders. She was paralyzed. No one had ever been so bold, and yet she was mesmerized by his sensual caresses. Samantha couldn't have protested if she'd wanted to, but she realized she didn't want to.

"Your hair is beautiful. It's a shame to put it up." His voice was rough with passion.

She drew in a deep breath but couldn't seem to fill her lungs. "It's so hot. It's cooler up."

His mouth descended toward hers slowly. His fingers slipped again into her hair as his mouth came down on hers in a gentle kiss, a feathery brush across her lips. Then his hands glided down her back to mold her against him, his hips trapping her between him and the door as his mouth covered hers with an enticing force.

When his tongue parted her lips, she welcomed him into her honeyed cavern. Her tongue met and parried with his, a sensuous dance between them, circling, thrusting, tasting.

Their hearts beat as one, like a jungle drum. Their breaths mingled, like the two mighty rivers at Manaus. Their hands discovered, like explorers in the virginal Amazon.

When he pulled away, his labored breathing attested to the effect she had on him. "I think I'd better say good-night, Sam."

How could he even think after that kiss? she wondered as she watched in a dreamlike state while he put distance between them.

"Yes, you're right," she murmured, realizing she was lying. She hadn't wanted the kiss to end.

Across the hall he waited while she unlocked her door. Her lips still tingled where his had been only a moment ago. She managed to let herself into her room without collapsing, but the second the door was closed, she leaned back against it for support.

That was when she saw him, a man peering in through her window.

She screamed.

CHAPTER FOUR

For a timeless second the man on the balcony and Samantha stared at each other. Then another scream ripped from her throat and the man fled.

"Sam, let me in!" Brock pounded on the locked door behind her.

She couldn't move.

Brock threw his body against the door and the wood splintered near the lock. "Sam!"

The force of Brock's body against the door a second time propelled Samantha into action. She couldn't afford to replace the door, and the clerk downstairs would charge her an arm and leg for it. She swung the door open and Brock raced into the room.

Stopping in the middle, he spun around, poised and ready to do battle. When he saw only Samantha, he faced her, confused. Was she one of those women who got hysterical over the slightest thing, despite her assurances to the contrary?

"Why did you scream?" He relaxed his taut muscles.

Samantha raised a trembling arm and pointed to the balcony door. "A man—a man was looking into the room."

Brock pivoted and strode to the balcony door, throwing it open. If there had been anyone out here, she certainly would have scared him away with her screams. After scanning the balcony in both directions once more, he started to turn back into the room, not convinced there had been anyone on the balcony. Then he saw a cigar butt by his foot. He bent over and picked it up. It was still smoldering, obviously having been discarded only moments before.

When he reentered the room, a frown creased his brow. "Whoever was here is gone now. I found this, though." He held up the cigar butt for her to look at.

Seeing the cigar butt explained the smell of cheap tobacco that permeated the air. It also meant that the man had obviously been inside her room. She eased down onto the only thing to sit on in the room, the bed.

Samantha was quaking so badly that Brock could see it. He put the cigar out in the ashtray on the table and sat beside her, drawing her against him. "He wouldn't dare come back tonight, Sam."

She buried her head into his shoulder, feeling safe with him so close. "I'm scared."

"That's perfectly normal," he whispered while stroking her.

"What if he does come back?"

"He won't. I'm sure your screams frightened him. They sure as hell gave me a scare."

Samantha smiled and lifted her face to look up into his. "You should hear me scream when I'm watching a scary movie on television. Of course, I refrain from doing it at the movies, but at home I think it's my way of letting off steam."

He smiled down at her. "Now, that would be an interesting sight. Do your neighbors ever complain?"

"Not yet."

"Tell you what, Sam. I'll make the calls to the hospitals tomorrow morning. I'll stay the night here in your room."

"Here!" Her voice was squeaky and her eyes widened as her mind raced with thoughts of him in her bedroom.

"On the floor, of course." His grin was crooked and there was laughter in his voice. "Unless . . ."

"No, the floor is fine," she replied quickly, relieved that she wouldn't have to spend the night alone. She needed her sleep, and now at least she would be able to get some—she hoped. She would just have to stop her mind from visualizing her and Brock alone. . . .

"Let me get a few things from my room. I won't be gone long. Lock the door after me."

"Does the lock still work?" she quipped.

"If it doesn't, just scream. I'll hear you."

The first ten minutes that Brock was gone, Samantha's eyes were glued to the balcony door. She was certain the man would materialize again despite Brock's assurances otherwise. Was that man on the balcony the one responsible for her brother's disappearance? How long had he been in the room? Why was he spying on her? Had he taken anything?

Samantha forced herself to look away from the balcony door and assess if anything was missing or misplaced. Everything seemed to be in order. Then she thought of Mark's suitcase. Quickly she knelt on the floor and searched under the bed. It was still there. She pulled it out and examined the piece of luggage. It was locked and appeared as it had earlier. With her teeth gritted she tugged on the handle, trying to open the suitcase. She glanced around for something to use to pry it open.

There was a knock on the door.

Samantha jumped, hurriedly slipping Mark's suitcase back under the bed.

"It's me, Sam."

When she heard Brock's voice, she sagged

with relief. Her nerves were stretched to their limit, she realized, as she went to the door to let Brock in.

He carried a pillow and blanket as well as a few toilet articles and immediately proceeded to make up a bed on the floor. Samantha watched, transfixed by his movements, a study in concise action. What would she have done earlier if Brock Slader hadn't helped her with the hotel clerk? She shuddered thinking about it.

When he was through, he straightened and glanced over at her. She was so still and pale-looking that he asked, "Are you all right?"

"I think so. But so much has happened in the last week. . . ." She swayed, her mind spinning.

Instantly his arm was about her, supporting her as he led her to the bed. "You're emotionally and physically exhausted. You need to sleep. We'll talk in the morning. I'll be right here, so you'll be safe."

He pulled back the sheet, and with her clothes still on, Samantha sank down onto the lumpy bed, oblivious to the world within seconds. . . .

Samantha ran toward the jungle, the pounding footsteps behind her closing in. The plants and vines enclosed her in a world of semidarkness, their branches clawing at her clothes as she tore through the dense foliage in her attempt to evade the men following her. With each step she gasped for air, her lungs burning.

Then suddenly the jungle was no longer surrounding her. She entered a clearing and stopped for a few seconds; but the footsteps grew even louder. Frantically she scanned the clearing for a way to escape as she rushed toward the opposite side. Plunging back into the thick undergrowth, she had only gone a few yards when she came to an abrupt halt at a cliff overlooking a river and a waterfall.

Looking across the raging river, she saw her brother and Brock beckoning to her. Behind her she heard her pursuers, the sound of their footsteps growing louder. Without thinking, she jumped. . . .

"No!" Samantha bolted upright in the bed at the Grand Hotel, drenched with sweat. She blinked, her heart still racing with the memories of her nightmare.

"Sam, what's wrong?" Brock asked, suddenly standing next to the bed.

"Bad dream," she replied in a quivering voice, smoothing her hair away from her face and taking deep breaths to calm herself.

Brock switched on the light and sat down next to her. She gazed for a few seconds into his sleepy eyes and saw tenderness in their gray depths; she went into his comforting arms. She realized it was becoming a habit she liked. He made her feel safe.

"Want to talk about it?"

The nightmare had seemed so real only a moment ago, but now with his arms about her, listening to his steady heartbeat against her ear, she realized the dream was just her over-tired mind at work. "I was being chased by some people in the jungle. They cornered me at a waterfall. You and Mark were on the other side waving for me to jump. I did. I don't swim very well." She shivered, recalling the dark water closing over her head as she hit the river. She feared drowning; that was how her father had died when she was a child.

"You jumped into a river at a waterfall?"

She laughed shakily. "You know how crazy dreams can be. I'm not responsible for the content of my nightmares."

"I'd say crazy was an apt description."

She pulled away from the security of his arms and stared at him for a long moment. She knew what she had to do. The answers to her brother's disappearance was at the Para Mission. Could she trust Brock Slader to take her there? Would he take her if she asked?

"I need your help."

"We've already been through that, Sam."

She held up her hand. "Please listen to my proposition before you refuse."

He sighed. "Okay."

"I have to go to the Para Mission." She hesitated for a moment, wondering again if she should trust him with the truth. If he was going to be her guide, she would be putting her life into his hands. She'd better trust him. "When my brother called, he told me there was something of great value there."

Brock's eyes narrowed. "The mission is a big compound."

"I think I can locate it when I get there," she hedged. "But the point is that if you'll take me to the place, I'll give you five percent of what's there."

"I'll do it for fifteen."

"Ten."

"Deal." He chuckled. "And you're wise not to trust completely, Sam. The less you reveal the better off you are."

She tilted her head to one side, regarding him intensely. "Why are you helping me now? I don't know for sure what Mark was referring to. I do know he's in big trouble because of it."

Brock shrugged. "I suppose it's the challenge. Searching Manaus isn't my idea of fun, but a treasure hunt is. And who knows? Your brother might have hit upon something big. Someone is after him. The Amazon is filled with riches if a person knows where to look."

Samantha was both disappointed and happy: disappointed because Brock was only going for the challenge and riches promised and happy because he was taking her. Maybe Mark had returned to the mission and she would find him

69

there. Then this brief interlude in paradise would be over and she could go back to New Orleans and her real life.

"When do you want to leave for the Para Mission?" Brock asked.

"As soon as possible. Tomorrow morning?"

"I have a friend I can borrow a bush plane from for a fee."

"Okay. Make whatever arrangements are necessary." Samantha mentally reviewed her dwindling bank account. Whom would she call when she needed money to get out of Manaus?

"Then we'll leave as soon as I can get things arranged. We can reach the mission in a few hours by plane. If there's no trouble, we should only need his plane for two days."

"Trouble?" She paled. Her life had been turned upside down in a space of a week and she wasn't even sure why. What was at the mission?

He reached up and framed her face with his hands. "Sam, someone is after what your brother stashed at the mission. I'd rather be prepared for trouble than not." His thumbs rubbed sensual circles on her neck, and his eyes met hers with a look that made her want to melt into him, become a part of this puzzling man.

"When I get my hands on my brother, he's going to get a piece of my mind," she said nervously, praying she would get her hands on

Mark. She sensed Brock's doubt that she would ever see her brother again. Fear dulled her eyes to a murky brown.

Brock started to speak, but Samantha put her finger over his mouth.

"No, don't say it. I know there's a chance I won't see him again. But I'm an optimist. I have to believe I will." Again she glimpsed sorrow in his eyes and wondered who had put it there.

"I know. I wish it could be different."

"Why?"

He looked toward the balcony door, his thoughts on the distant past. "I told you I had a sister. Her husband, my best friend all through high school, has been missing in action in Vietnam for sixteen years. She still keeps hoping he's alive and will come home one day. She's placed her life on hold." He looked back at Samantha, his sorrow evident in the grim lines of his face. "I know the hell my sister went through, is still going through, not knowing for sure one way or another. Of course, if she were given a choice, she'd want her husband home alive. But she wasn't given a choice, and you may not have one, either, Sam. I guess earlier today I was just trying to warn you, prepare you for what may happen."

Her throat ached; she wanted to erase the sorrow from his eyes. "You're close to your sister like I am with Mark."

"We're twins. It's uncanny how at times one of us can tell what the other is thinking."

"You don't think Mark is alive, do you?"

Silence seemed to make the humid air even thicker. Samantha held her breath, waiting for his answer.

"The longer he's missing . . ."

"You haven't answered my question."

His gaze swerved to her and pinned her in a relentless hold. "No, Sam, I don't."

Samantha closed her eyes, wanting to deny the possible truth in Brock's words. She felt his touch on her shoulders; she allowed him to draw her to his chest.

"It's not important what I think. I've been wrong in the past and I hope I'm wrong about this."

"You have to be," she whispered against his bare chest, the heat of his body warding off the chill she suddenly felt.

Brock lounged back against the headboard, cradling Samantha against him, his hand caressing her arm. "We have a long day ahead of us. Try to get some sleep," he murmured against the top of her head.

She listened to his steady heartbeat, its soothing rhythm lulling her with its sense of peace, security. Her eyelids drifted closed. Did she imagine him kissing her hair? she wondered as sleep descended.

Sunlight poured in through the balcony

door, heating the room to a stifling temperature only an hour after dawn. With her body sprawled face down on the bed, Samantha felt the warmth of the sun on her left cheek and forced herself to open her eyes, though her whole being protested the rude awakening.

It took a moment for her to remember where she was, but one glimpse of the shabby room, and she instantly recalled everything about the night before—Brock's kiss, the man peering in through the window, her nightmare, Brock's arms about her as she fell asleep a second time.

She shot up in bed and looked around for Brock, who to her relief was sleeping soundly on the floor. Sighing, she sank back down onto the mattress and gave herself some time to fully awaken. At home it always took a good thirty minutes before her mind began to function in the morning.

"Good morning, Sam."

She gasped and twisted her head toward Brock, who towered over her. She hadn't even heard him move!

When she didn't say anything, his mouth slowly curved into a positively sexy smile that no man should have a right to own.

"This is morning, I believe"—he glanced out the balcony door—"and if we're successful and find what your brother hid, it will be a good day."

73

"Hello, how are you?" What a ridiculous thing to say after spending the night with him in the same room! But that's what happened when she only had five minutes to awaken.

His smile broadened. "Fine. We'd better get a move on. There's a lot that has to be done before we leave. I'll need to make those calls to the hospitals as well as my friend. Pack light for a couple of days in the jungle. What kind of clothes did you bring?"

Samantha stared wide eyed at him. He was clicking off things to do so fast she was having a hard time keeping up, even as organized as she usually was.

"Clothes, Sam?" The gleam in his eyes brightened.

"Oh! Uh, a few sundresses, sandals, a pair of jeans, and a short-sleeve shirt. And shorts."

"In your suitcase?"

She nodded. She hadn't had time to unpack the day before.

Before she realized his intention he had her suitcase on the bed and was starting to open it. She scrambled to a kneeling position and banged it closed, nearly smashing his fingers.

He glanced up at her with amusement in his eyes. "Sam, we have very little time if we want to get to the mission by dark. From your description it sounds as though you have nothing appropriate for the jungle. Rio, maybe, but not here."

"Do you always take charge without asking?"

"Since I'm taking you to the mission, yes. Since I've traveled in the jungle and you haven't, yes."

She practically sat on her suitcase to prevent him from looking inside. The very top item was a lacy bra and panties. When she had purchased them in New Orleans, she had bought the saleswoman's line about a woman having silky, pretty underwear next to her skin to make her feel confident and good about herself. "What kind of clothes do you suggest I take?"

"Cotton pants and a long-sleeve shirt in a light color. They should fit loosely. And good sturdy shoes."

"Why? We won't have to hike. And long sleeves in this heat?"

"I told you I always travel prepared for any kind of situation. You have to in the jungle. Tennis shoes will do. And the long sleeves are for protection against the sun and insects." He gathered up his few possessions and started for the door.

"Where are you going? What am I suppose to do about clothes? I don't have anything like that."

At the door he turned back and replied, "I'm going to get ready and make the calls downstairs. Then I'll be back to pick you up for breakfast and a quick shopping trip. I need to get a few items too. Wear one of those sundresses for the time being." He opened the door.

"Wait!"

Brock paused in the doorway.

Sitting on her suitcase reminded Samantha of her brother's still unopened one under her bed. Maybe there was a clue to his disappearance in it. She slipped from the top of her suitcase and started to retrieve Mark's.

"Sam, we're wasting valuable time." Brock glanced back at her, her bottom sticking up in the air as she searched for something under the bed. "As much as I appreciate the delightful picture you present, I have a lot to do before we can leave."

She slid Mark's suitcase out from under the bed. "I need you to open this." Straightening, she dropped the piece of luggage down on the mattress.

"You mean you haven't? That should have been done first thing."

"It's locked." She wasn't about to mention that with his presence in the room she had forgotten all about the suitcase.

Brock walked back to the bed and took five seconds with his pocket knife to open it.

"Where did you learn that?" Samantha asked, astonished at how easy he made it look.

She would never bother to lock her luggage again when she traveled!

"Around." He flipped back the suitcase top and rummaged through Mark's belongings, then checked the lining, but there was nothing in it to indicate what had happened to her brother. "I didn't think he'd put anything important in this, then leave it behind, but it had to be ruled out." Brock closed the suitcase. "Now, I'm going. If we're lucky, we'll manage to be out of here by dark."

CHAPTER FIVE

At three o'clock Samantha was seated in the small bush plane with Brock, waiting for him to take off. Dressed in cotton pants and a loose fitting, long sleeve, white blouse, she had to admit it was comfortable and as cool as possible in Manaus's staggering heat. She had also purchased another, similar shirt along with a wide-brimmed hat and a pair of tennis shoes. She had packed the extra shirt for her trip to the mission in a new canvas bag that was easier to carry than her or Mark's suitcase, which she had left with the clerk at the Grand Hotel—for a price, of course.

What had disconcerted Samantha about their shopping trip was that Brock had bought weapons, a machete, a knife, and a gun. They were going to a mission run by priests and he was carrying a damn arsenal!

Finally they were given clearance to take off. Samantha braced herself for it and closed her eyes. Flying was right up there with exercising as one of her least favorite things to do, especially when the plane looked as if it had flown in World War II.

"We're up in the air now. You can open your eyes," Brock said, laughter tinging his voice.

Annoyed at his amusement, she asked, "Are you afraid of anything?"

"Yes. Women like you."

"Women like me? What does that mean?"

"Helpless."

"Helpless! I'll have you know I've been on my own for years and have done very well."

"Yes, back where you come from you probably have," he admitted, "but here you're totally out of your element."

She couldn't argue with that. Ever since she had walked into the Grand Hotel and he had helped her with the desk clerk, she had been dependent on him—something that was as alien to her as the environment she was in, the situation she was in, and the man she was with.

"I'm not a hero, Sam. I don't make a habit of rescuing people."

"Then why did you rescue me yesterday at the hotel? You could have ignored my predicament with the desk clerk."

He wasn't sure how to answer her, so he remained quiet. He kneaded the coiled muscles of his neck and shoulder. His body was stiff from sleeping on the hard floor.

"Why, Brock?" she persisted.

"For the life of me I don't know," he finally answered with a wry smile. "Let's just chalk it up to helping a fellow American." He spared her a quick, probing look. "A pretty one at that."

Samantha blushed and diverted her gaze. Finally she got up the courage to lean close to the side window and look down. A few hundred feet below was a blanket of green extending as far as she could see. Occasionally the green was broken by a brown ribbon of water or a flight of some vividly colored birds. Sprinkled among the green were the golden canopies of vochysia trees, often two hundred feet across.

When Brock pointed to a waterfall below, Samantha was reminded of her nightmare the night before as she watched the churning water plunge into the ravine. Leaving the relative civilization of Manaus behind and entering the world of the primitive, hostile jungle made her nightmare come back in full force. She began to wonder if she would ever see Manaus—or even New Orleans—again. She shivered.

"You can't be cold. It must be ninety degrees."

She was surprised that Brock was so attuned to her every movement. There was nothing casual about the man; he was always keenly alert even when he seemed relaxed.

"That waterfall reminded me of my dream."

He placed a hand on her thigh and squeezed

her leg reassuringly. "Believe me, I would never motion for you to jump into a raging river right before a waterfall."

"It seemed so real."

"Dreams often are. Forget it. That waterfall back there is the closest you'll come to seeing one," he replied in a voice that he hoped sounded convincing. He had learned one thing in the jungle: Anything could happen.

"Everything looks the same to me, green. How can you tell where you're going?" she asked to change the subject.

"By certain landmarks, usually rivers, sometimes mountain ranges."

"How long have you been in the Amazon?"

"Long enough."

"Where are you from?"

"Houston."

"Oh, that's not too far from where I live, New Orleans."

"Practically neighbors," he teased, giving her a brief smile before again falling silent.

Samantha got the impression he wasn't one for small talk or he didn't like the subject— himself. She supposed when a person traveled in the jungle he got out of the habit of conversing to pass the time.

Over two hours later and several failed attempts to discover more about Brock, Samantha saw the clearing and mission come into view. Brock circled once, then started his descent toward the small strip of jungle that had been cleared for a runway.

As they landed, Samantha forced herself to keep her eyes open. She wished she hadn't. The wheels hit ground, but they continued racing toward the end of the runway and the wall of green trees. It seemed hours later before the plane started to slow down. Samantha was sure they were going to crash into the jungle, and for the hundredth time she wondered what insanity had prompted her to come to the Amazon.

Two feet from the wall of trees they came to a stop. Samantha released her death grip on the seat and tore her gaze from the jungle in front of the plane to look at Brock. That familiar silver flash in his eyes made her fume.

"Short runway," he commented offhandedly as he prepared to leave the plane. "Some guy over there wasn't as lucky."

Samantha looked toward the place he indicated and gasped. Not far from them was a plane that had collided into the wall of trees. Vines were beginning to grow around it, and she realized the jungle would soon absorb the foreign object.

"I didn't want to tell you earlier that landing can be tricky at these places. Usually the bare minimum of runway is cleared and kept in some kind of condition for planes."

"Thanks," she muttered, wiping the sweat

from her forehead and neck with a handkerchief. She wasn't sure if it was from the heat or
her nerves, but her blouse was soaking wet.

As they were climbing down from the plane,
Samantha saw another plane parked to the side
of the runway. Then she noticed a priest walking toward them. Brock tossed down their bags
and hopped off the wing to greet the man.

"I'm Father Carlos." He offered his hand to
Brock.

"I've heard a lot about you, Father." Brock
shook the older man's hand. "I'm Brock Slader,
and this is Samantha Prince."

"Pleased to meet you." Samantha placed her
hand in the priest's. As they shook hands, she
felt uncomfortable under Father Carlos' intent
gaze. It must be the after effects from the landing, she decided, her legs still feeling wobbly
on solid ground.

"What can I do for you?" Father Carlos
asked.

"We need a place to stay for the night,"
Brock said, cutting in before Samantha could
ask about her brother.

"Of course. You are welcome to use Para Mission for as long as you like. We don't get very
many Americans here. Father Paul will be
thrilled to see fellow countrymen." He began
to walk toward the compound. "You must
freshen up for dinner and join us. I want to

83

know the latest from the United States. We hear so little out here in the jungle."

"Why didn't you let me ask about Mark?" Samantha whispered while Father Carlos paused to say something to a native.

"Not yet. Patience."

Samantha was shown to her room in a house in the center of the compound, obviously used by Father Carlos. Brock and the priest left her to freshen up. As Samantha was freshening up, she wondered where Brock was staying. She was nervous; she supposed from the anticipation and excitement.

There was a basin of water that she used to sponge herself off, and by the time she had changed into her other shirt, she did feel a little better. The sun had set rapidly while she had been cleaning up and the air was cooler as she went in search of Brock and Father Carlos.

She found them in the living room. They both stood as she entered and both appraised her as she walked over to a chair. In Brock's eyes there was a look of male appreciation; Father Carlos's gaze held a calculated shrewdness. It was obvious he was wondering why a woman like her would be in the Amazon, Samantha thought. She was wondering the very same thing.

"As I was telling Mr. Slader here, we don't get many visitors this way. What brings you to the mission?" Father Carlos asked Samantha.

Remembering what Brock had said about not mentioning her brother yet, Samantha couldn't think of a good lie to tell Father Carlos.

Brock interceded, saying, "Samantha is a zoologist studying the anaconda. We're flying back to Manaus tomorrow."

"Have you been successful, Miss Prince?"

"Yes," she murmured. Studying snakes? Of all the creatures in the jungle for Brock to come up with, the anaconda was certainly the last one she would have picked. Why couldn't it have been the beautiful, sleek jaguar? She would even have settled for the capybara, the largest rodent in the world. Samantha hated snakes.

Father Carlos stood and excused himself for a moment.

"I can't even abide a small garter snake, let alone a snake over twenty feet long," Samantha said the second the priest had left.

Brock laughed. "Sorry. That was the first thing I came up with."

"Where are you staying?"

A frown dimmed the silver light in Brock's eyes. "In the house next door. Father Carlos told me he and another priest from the United States, the Father Paul he spoke of, stay in this house, so there's no more room."

"Do you think I should ask him about Mark now?"

"No," came the instant reply.

"Maybe Mark has been back here or maybe he's here now."

"The less anyone knows the better, Sam."

Brock's vehemence puzzled Samantha. She started to protest, but just then Father Carlos returned with the same native he had talked to earlier. Her eyes grew round and her mouth went dry. The man was carrying an anaconda at least eight feet long.

"I regret that he's only a baby, but I'm sure you'll enjoy examining him nonetheless, Miss Prince."

Father Carlos waved the native forward, and Samantha pressed herself as far as she could into the chair, wishing she could somehow disappear. As the man towered above her with the thick, long snake wrapped about him, waiting for her to do something, she shot Brock a killing look.

He could hardly contain his amusement. Did anything nonplus that man? She would love to discover something that got under his skin.

"Miss Prince, is something wrong?" Father Carlos asked.

"Oh, no. I'm just speechless you have such a beautiful specimen." She hoped that sounded enough like a zoologist to appease the priest.

"Feel free to hold him."

She had known he was going to say that. As it was, the snake was too close for her already.

She swallowed several times and tried to think of a way out of this mess. She desperately glanced over at Brock for help, but he was too busy looking somewhere else. *Chicken,* she thought and moistened her parched throat again.

She forced herself to rise and reach out to touch the snake, all the time making sure her face didn't express the disgust and fear churning her stomach. She was surprised the skin felt dry, not wet or slimy, as it looked. A little braver, she stroked the anaconda, once, then twice, and felt her courage increase.

But when the native thrust the snake into her arms, she nearly screamed and backed away. The chair and the puzzled look on Father Carlos' face, however, stopped her. Fortifying herself with a deep breath, she gingerly took the snake and it immediately began coiling itself around her body. Had she come thousands of miles to be strangled to death by a snake?

Something in her expression must have triggered a spark of chivalry in Brock, for he interrupted her "examination" of the snake to take the anaconda from her, muttering something to the effect that he would love to look at it too. She gladly gave the snake to Brock.

With ease he handled the long snake, and Samantha was beginning to think nothing frightened the man. The anaconda was completely wrapped around him and he actually looked as if he was enjoying it!

When an Indian woman came to the doorway, Father Carlos announced, "Ah, I see our dinner is ready."

The native took the snake away, and such relief trembled through Samantha that she knew she would have collapsed if Brock hadn't been there to support her with an arm about her waist. She wanted to hit him for having put her into the situation in the first place, and she wanted to hug him for having rescued her from it. It seemed her feelings for Brock were always at odds.

Over dinner Samantha told Father Carlos the latest news from the United States and steered the conversation as far away from snakes and zoology as possible. Halfway through dinner they were joined by Father Paul, who was new to the mission, having arrived only recently, Father Carlos told Brock and Samantha.

Throughout the rest of the dinner Samantha often caught Father Paul's eyes on her. He made her feel uneasy, as if she were the specimen and he the zoologist. When the dinner was over, she was glad that Brock suggested they retire early for the night. He escorted her to her room.

"I'd invite you in for coffee, but I think our hosts might frown upon that. Father Paul kept giving me looks all through dinner. Do you suppose he doesn't approve of us traveling together, unmarried?" Samantha was trying to appear light and unconcerned, but her stomach was twisted into a huge knot. She really wished that Brock weren't a house away.

"We'll be gone by tomorrow afternoon."

"Brock, I . . ."

"What?"

"Oh, nothing," she lied. She had almost asked him to spend the night in her room again —on the floor, of course. But she had no right to ask him just because she was uncomfortable and edgy. She couldn't even tell him why, because she didn't know why she felt that way herself.

"Well, I guess this is good night then," he murmured, leaning closer, his hand braced against the wall next to her head.

"Yes, I guess it is." Her words came out in a breathless rush. His mouth was only inches from hers and she wanted him to kiss her again.

"We have to get up early," he whispered, lifting both hands to gently touch her throat slowly, deliberately. His eyes seemed absorbed in the movement of his fingertips as they stroked her sensitive skin, pausing to graze the hollow at the base of her throat.

Her pulse rate jumped alarmingly. His gaze whipped back to hers, as though they both were startled by her intense reaction to his caresses. Some new and indefinable tension laced the air between them.

"We really should get some sleep." He breathed the words against her lips right before claiming them in a deep kiss that brought her hands up to clutch his shoulders for support.

Her equilibrium suffered a further disruption when he trailed light kisses to her earlobe and began to nibble. Her world was upside down, and she was beginning to think Brock Slader was the cause of it rather than her brother's disappearance or the Amazon jungle.

"I'd better go." His words tickled her ear and neck. Reluctantly he placed her away from him. "Good night, Sam."

She watched him walk away, her hand brushing across her kiss-swollen lips. After Brock had disappeared around a corner, she stood in the hallway a moment longer, staring at nothing in particular. The humid air was saturated with the smell of damp foliage and tobacco.

She practically floated into her bedroom on a cloud of romantic dreams, but the laughter of Fathers Carlos and Paul pierced her haven, sharply reminding her of her quest. She closed the door, looked for a lock, and when she found none, she thought about putting the table or chest up against the door.

Their robust laughter drifted to her again,

and she tensed. Something was wrong. She felt it deep in her bones. Too restless to sleep, she dragged the chest over to block the door, then began to pace the small room.

Suddenly she stopped and whirled toward the door, her hand flying up to her mouth to silence a cry. Father Paul was the same man who had been out on her balcony! Out in the hallway the cheap cigar tobacco she had smelled had been the same as in her hotel room.

Her trembling quickly spread through her entire body. She sank down onto the bed and tried to think rationally. "It's impossible," she whispered into the silence. "He's a priest."

Why would a priest be spying in her room in Manaus? Though it made no sense and she had only caught a glimpse of the man on her balcony, she knew he was Father Paul. And with that she realized Brock and she were in danger.

Samantha snatched up her canvas bag and stuffed all her belongings back into it. She had to find Brock. She looked at the door, then at the window. The two priests were in the living room, and that was the only way out of the house except through her window.

Tossing her bag out the open window, Samantha climbed out, landing on her bottom in a bed of flowers. She pushed herself to her feet and allowed her eyes a moment to adjust to the moonlit night. The house next door was pitch black. She had no idea which room Brock was in, but she felt the urgency to get to him.

Glancing over her shoulder several times, she hurried in the moonlight toward the house. Once inside, she realized the design of this house was similar to the other. She decided to go to the room that would be hers in the other house, hoping that was where Brock was staying.

Samantha paused at the door, then slowly turned the knob and eased it open. Peering into the room, she saw the outline of a body in the bed and wedged herself through the small opening. She tiptoed toward the bed, her arms outstretched to prevent her from bumping into anything.

At the bed she reached down to touch the dark shape when a hand was clasped over her mouth, cutting off her breath. Something cold and metallic was thrust against her throat.

CHAPTER SIX

The icy touch of the knife against her throat paralyzed Samantha. She suddenly felt like the man in the fable who had a choice of two doors, one with a tiger behind it and the other with a beautiful woman behind it. She had obviously picked the tiger.

With one arm across her front, her assailant hauled her back against his broad chest. Samantha was so frightened she couldn't breathe. Whose room had she wandered into? Father Paul's?

"Shh, Sam. It's me." Brock loosened his hand from her mouth as the knife dropped away from her throat.

Samantha, inhaling deeply, slumped back into him. When she had filled her lungs, she spun around, her hands flying to her waist. "You could have warned me or something. I think I aged ten years in one minute."

"I didn't want to take the chance you might

scream. I've heard you before. I didn't want the whole compound awakened."

"Do you always try to shut up people with a knife at their throats?"

"I didn't know it was you at first. I told you I never take things for granted."

He grasped her arm with one hand and tugged her toward him while his other hand tilted up her chin, forcing her to look at him. Then, before she could say anything more, her soft lips were crushed mercilessly beneath his. His caressing fingers glided to the curve of her neck as his tongue pushed its way into her mouth to taunt her.

Sensations bombarded her with a stunning effect: the bristly feel of his day's growth of beard against her tender skin, the taste of him on her tongue, the warmth of his hands on her body as they roamed down the length of her back, the masculine scent of him that intoxicated her.

"To what do I owe the honor of this visit?" he asked, his breath fanning her cheek.

She ignored his husky tone. They didn't have any time to lose. Before she forgot why she had come to his room in the first place and surrendered to the dazzling pleasure he offered, she pulled out of his embrace, backing up against the bed.

"You don't have to worry if our being in the same bedroom will shock the dear fathers.

94

They aren't priests—at least I don't think they are. Father Paul was the man on my balcony."

"Well, that explains that nagging voice inside my head."

"Nagging voice?"

"When something doesn't quite ring true, I have a little nagging voice, a sixth sense some people call it, that warns me." His voice was businesslike now, all traces of the husky, passionate tone gone. "Did you notice how deserted the compound was when we arrived? It's possible Father Carlos isn't the real padre and that they're both involved with what's going on—whatever that is. From all I've heard concerning this mission, the real Father Carlos has his hands full. Too many Indians come for aid and there aren't enough workers to help."

"And we only saw two Indians, the cook and the one with the snake. By the way, when we get out of this mess, remind me to pay you back for that one."

"Come on." Chuckling, he took her hand and grabbed his backpack from the chair. "When we're safely back in Manaus, it will be a pleasure, Sam. Right now, I think we'd better get the hell out of here."

"But the treasure! We can't leave without it." She tugged her hand from his, standing her ground. They had come too far not to search for it.

"Where did your brother hide it?"

"Under the altar in the church."

"Great. That's across the compound from our plane. No one ever hides anything right next to the landing strip. Everything would be so much simpler," Brock muttered as he eased the door open and peered into the hallway.

"I wonder why they put you in this house."

"Have you ever heard of divide and conquer?"

A shiver streaked up her spine. "Do you think they'll try something during the night?"

He shot her a quick look over his shoulder as he led the way out of the house. "Yep, I'm afraid these men have been about as patient as they're going to be."

"I wonder where the real priests are."

Brock halted at the front door and turned toward her, gripping her arms and pulling her close. She thought he was going to kiss her again, and her feminine side welcomed it, even though they couldn't afford the time.

Instead, he whispered into her ear, "Sam, wonder about those things some other time."

"I always talk when I'm scared. The sound of my own voice calms me."

"In this case the sound of your voice will alert them." His words came out gently while his hands lessened their hold on her arms.

His mouth touched hers for a brief searing moment, then he released her to open the front door. That fleeting kiss left her wanting much more. What would it be like if they had met under normal circumstances? she wondered.

"Move!" Brock's furiously whispered order scattered her wandering thoughts and sharply brought her back to the situation at hand.

This was no time to daydream. She would need her full concentration if she was going to make it out of this place alive. Not for one moment did she think these men after Mark were out for a Sunday stroll. They were playing a deadly game, and they'd do anything to win.

Outside, backed against the front of the house, Brock took a minute to get his bearings. Samantha, next to him, dared not move. She heard the laughter from inside the other house where the two fake priests were, for she was sure now they weren't real priests. It sounded as if they were having their fill of some *cachaca*. Maybe they would get drunk and forget all about Brock and herself.

Without a word Brock grasped her hand again and motioned for her to follow him. They ran from dark shadow to dark shadow until they were at the small white New England–style church. It seemed incongruous and stood alone, a bit of civilization in the midst of a vast, untamed wilderness.

The door creaked when Brock inched it open. To Samantha it sounded as if the church bells were pealing, announcing their presence to the whole compound. She looked back several times to see if the two fake priests had heard. Thankfully the yard was empty.

Moonlight streamed in through the windows on the sides of the church, affording them enough light to see where they were going as they made their way toward the altar. But even in the moonlight Samantha managed to catch her foot on a wooden bench, causing it to scrape forward. She halted, her heavy breathing the only sound disturbing the church's eerie quiet now.

Rubbing her damp palms together, she continued toward the altar, deciding she could never be a thief or a spy. Her body wasn't cut out to take this kind of tension—or physical abuse.

Suddenly Brock stopped and Samantha collided against his back. He placed his hand over her mouth to stifle her gasp of surprise and dragged her quickly down a row of benches until they were wedged between the wall and a wardrobe closet that shielded them from the back of the church.

Brock slowly took his hand from her mouth, but she knew better than to say a word. His tension was conveyed by every taut muscle in his body.

It wasn't until a minute later, though, that Samantha heard the men's voices and was amazed at Brock's keen hearing. Her heart had been beating so loudly that that was about all she could hear. And her breathing sounded so labored that she wondered if she were directing the men right to their hiding place.

The door at the back of the church opened and Samantha froze.

"Paul, what are you doing going in there? We've got work to do," Father Carlos said in English.

"I thought I heard something."

Father Carlos came to the door and looked into the dark church. "Probably one of those damn natives sneaking back here after we told them to get lost. Hurry if you must take a look. Our Mr. Slader is waiting."

"Then Miss Prince," Paul said with a cackle that chilled Samantha in the heat of the jungle. "I think I'm going to like talking to her."

The men were going to find them and she didn't know the first thing about fighting, Samantha thought frenetically. Why didn't she pay attention when Friday-night wrestling was on the television?

Paul stepped into the church. Samantha's heart stopped beating; her breathing was suspended in her lungs. But instead of walking farther down the aisle, Paul swung his flashlight in a wide arc, illuminating the dark shadows. Samantha and Brock flattened themselves even more against the wall.

A trickle of sweat rolled down her face, then

another. The light shone near the closet, only two inches from Brock's arm. It seemed to linger there for an eternity. It took all of Samantha's willpower not to cry out in fright.

"There's no one here. Let's get going, Paul."

Paul mumbled something, clicked off his flashlight, and left the church.

Samantha slowly released her pent-up breath, sagging against Brock.

Silently Brock took her hand again, and they hurried toward the altar. It wouldn't take the two men long to discover Brock was missing. Paul would then remember the noise he thought he had heard in the church and be back to investigate more thoroughly.

At first they fumbled in the dim light, trying to feel for anything under the altar or on the earthen floor that might be a treasure. But they couldn't find anyplace that might hide something of value.

"Maybe I misunderstood my brother. This is just a wooden slab," Samantha whispered in disappointment as her hands again ran over the planks that were used to make the altar.

"I'd hoped I wouldn't have to use this." Brock rummaged in his backpack and extracted a small flashlight that looked like a pen. "It won't matter in a few minutes. The good fathers will know we've flown the coop."

Brock examined the space under the altar until he spotted a crack in the wooden-planked table. He pried it loose and a small black book fell onto the hard-packed dirt floor. "Could something of value be your brother's black book?" One thick brow rose in bewilderment. "Like the next man, I like a pretty woman, but to risk my life for ten percent of a little black book seems a bit much to ask. Don't you think, Sam?"

Samantha picked up the book and flipped through it, ignoring Brock's tone. The writing didn't make sense. It was in some kind of code. She showed it to Brock. "What do you think?"

A noise in the compound demanded his attention. "I think we'd better get moving before all hell breaks out."

Samantha stuffed the book into her canvas bag. There would be time later to go over it, if they made it out alive. The shouts in the compound were louder, only yards away.

"The church!" someone yelled.

"What do we do now?" Samantha tried to keep the panic from her voice, but the only kind of danger she had ever had to face was an irate customer who felt she had been cheated. Samantha would gladly settle for being back in New Orleans now, confronting that woman with her umbrella raised, ready to fight to the end for her two dollars.

The sound of pounding footsteps grew louder at the back of the church. Brock took a few seconds to assess their situation, then seized Samantha's hand and ran for the side window. It was open and he dived through it, followed by Samantha, who landed on top of him, knocking her breath out. Several men burst into the church as Samantha rolled off Brock and scrambled to her feet, dragging air into her lungs.

"It won't take them long to discover the broken plank of wood," Brock whispered, crouching behind a bush at the side of the church.

He examined the open compound. They would have to cross it to get to their plane; they didn't have time to go along the outskirts of the mission. He didn't like the odds that were stacking up against them. This wasn't at all the way he had planned it in Manaus.

Brock turned to Samantha and cupped her face to get her full attention. He could sense her fear as though it were tangible. "Listen. We have to make a run for the plane." He gestured toward the yard. "Across there."

"But they'll see us."

"Probably. But it's our only chance to get to the plane before they do." He prepared to make a run. "How were you at the hundred-yard dash?"

"Lousy."

With that they started to race across the compound. Earlier that day it hadn't seemed very big, but now the yards between them and

102

the plane seemed like miles, and Samantha's legs couldn't keep up with Brock's longer ones.

A shout behind them momentarily caused Samantha to falter. Then the sound of gunfire and a bullet whizzing by her head propelled her across the yard. She had seen it countless times in the movies, but her life wasn't supposed to be like that. The movies were fantasy, the guns only firing blanks, but the men after them were firing *real* bullets. A bullet struck the dirt near her foot, scattering the earth in clouds of dust, and she ran faster.

A few feet in front Brock slowed, his eyes scanning the dark terrain near the planes. With the runway so short their chances at night were slim. Suddenly he altered his direction and ran toward the jungle near the edge of the landing strip, glancing back to make sure that Samantha was following.

When he plunged into the total darkness of the trees, he waited for Samantha, taking her hand—it was becoming such a natural thing to do—before moving deeper into the dense foliage. He put his fingers over her mouth to indicate the need for quiet. He knew she had a hundred questions for him, but the time to answer them wasn't now.

They went several hundred yards into the jungle before Brock found a tree to climb. He motioned Samantha to go up the trunk first, his ears attuned to the slightest unnatural noise.

Secured in the branches of a large tree, they were about fifteen feet off the ground. He situated himself next to Samantha and put his arm around her. She was trembling.

"We're safe," he whispered into her ear.

Safe? Two stories up in a tree? She wasn't a cat, and she realized how precarious their perch was when she tried to move to make herself more comfortable.

"You weren't hit, were you?" Brock asked when she didn't say anything, which wasn't like her one bit.

She shook her head and molded herself even more into the curve of his arm. "Why are we here?"

The night sounds of the jungle masked their whispers, so Brock took a chance to explain his decision, "I don't think we could have made it taking off at night from that runway."

"I'm not sure that's what you should call it," she said with a shaky laugh.

"We'll have to wait till dawn, then take our chances on getting back to the plane."

"But surely they'll be guarding it."

"No doubt. But I believe the risks are less at dawn than now. Try and get some sleep. To-morrow will be one hell of a day."

Samantha was exhausted, but there was no way she could have slept, even in Brock's arms. Her eyes were wide and constantly surveying the jungle for any signs of the men from the mission, or even a predator who hunted at night. Didn't jaguars live in trees and hunt their food at night?

"Relax, Sam. It will be hours." Brock kneaded the tightness in her shoulders.

"You sound like running for your life is an everyday occurrence for you."

"No, but I have had a few brushes. When you go into uncharted territory, that happens occasionally."

"Uncharted territory?"

He tensed, again laying his fingers over her mouth. For a few minutes Samantha couldn't tell any sound that was different from the constant chorus of insects. Then she heard the slashing sound. Some men from the compound were heading toward their tree!

The sound of their machetes cutting the foliage stopped. One of them cursed.

Paul—Samantha would know his gruff voice anywhere—said, "We can't find anything out here in the dark. We'll track them tomorrow. They won't go very far."

"No, Miss Prince won't be able to escape us like her brother. I've taken care of that."

Samantha felt a momentary lift in her spirits. *Mark had escaped!* That meant he was still alive—if something or someone else hadn't gotten him.

The two men's voices faded as they headed back to the mission. Samantha's spirits plummeted when she evaluated their situation, which didn't look one bit promising. "They will be back tomorrow morning."

"And we won't be here." Brock leaned back against the tree and pulled Samantha against him. "Sam, at least close your eyes and rest. I need you in top condition tomorrow. I won't mislead you. It will be damn hard getting out of here."

"What if they did something to the plane?"

"They need their plane. We'll take that if we have to. And if we can't, then we'll walk out of here. You'll do what's necessary."

She followed his gentle command and closed her eyes, willing her body to relax against his strength. At least they were safe for the next few hours. Her exhaustion swept through her, and she eased into a deep sleep, comforted by Brock's even breathing and steady heartbeat.

Someone was shaking her. Even though her bed felt so hard, she didn't want to get up. "Sam! We've got to get going and be in place at dawn."

The urgency in Brock's voice roused her completely. She forced herself to leave the security of his arms and climb down from their tree. Near the bottom a branch dug into her leg, and she bit her lower lip to keep from crying out. It was still dark in the jungle, the canopy of trees blocking out all light, even from the moon. But she felt a trickle of blood run down her leg and knew it wasn't just a scratch.

Silently, like a night prowler, Brock moved forward toward what Samantha supposed was the landing strip. She was so completely turned around that she didn't know which way she was going. Her leg throbbed where the branch had speared her, but she kept up with Brock.

At the edge of the jungle Brock halted and crouched down to evaluate their chances, peering through the foliage. There were two men with rifles guarding the plane, their bodies silhouetted against the gray light of dawn. Both planes looked untouched.

"We need to create a diversion," Brock whispered. "Any ideas?"

"An explosion?"

"And how do you suggest doing that?"

"You mean you aren't carrying dynamite in your backpack? I always thought you came prepared."

He smiled. "Maybe a fire will do. I do have matches."

"Wait! Did you notice the gas-powered generator next to the house? If we can set fire to that, then the gasoline in it will explode."

"I like that, Sam." He started forward.

She grabbed his arm. "Where are you going?"

"To blow up the generator, general."

"Not without me."

"Listen, I'm all for togetherness, but if I get caught you still have a chance to get away. Besides, when the generator goes, I want you to get inside the plane. When I come running, there will be no time to waste."

"What about the other plane?"

"I'll take care of it."

"What are you trying to be? A hero? I thought that wasn't your bag of tea."

He brushed his finger down her jawline, the look in his eyes incredibly tender. "I'm just trying to keep both of us alive. There's nothing heroic in that." Then in a brisker tone, he added, "Now, follow orders."

"I think I've just been demoted to private," she muttered as Brock headed along the edge of the compound toward the house and the generator.

The gray tint of dawn began to turn to a rosy hue in the eastern sky as Samantha waited, counting each second that Brock was gone. Though she knew he intended to blow up the generator, when the noise thundered in the air, she jumped, her heartbeat accelerating quickly.

The explosion was her signal to move, but for a minute Samantha's gaze was fixed upon the billowing flames that leapt toward the heavens. It was seeing the two guards hurrying toward the fire that finally impelled her to run to the plane. Crouched low, she scrambled up onto

108

the wing and practically fell into the copilot's seat.

After strapping herself in, she scanned the area for Brock, praying he made it out alive, because she knew in her heart without him she had no chance to make it back to Manaus. She didn't even know which way to go, let alone how to fly a plane!

Fifty heartbeats later she saw Brock climb onto the wing and thrust the cockpit door open. He got into the pilot's seat and started the plane.

"Any problems?" she asked.

"Yes, them." He tossed his head in the direction of the two priests rushing toward the plane with their guns firing.

One bullet struck the wing of the plane on Samantha's side. She stared at the hole it made and thought of all the dull things she would love to be doing right now in New Orleans.

Brock turned the plane around and began to taxi down the short runway. The sound of the gunfire ricocheted through Samantha's mind as more bullets hit the plane. They picked up speed, the dense jungle wall at the end of the runway coming closer and closer. Only a few yards away from the tree barrier the nose of the plane lifted, followed by the wheels, then the tail. They were airborne, passing several feet over the tops of the trees.

"We made it!" Samantha exclaimed, wanting

to throw her arms around Brock and kiss him for pulling it off.

"And they shouldn't be following. I removed the spark plugs from their plane before setting off the generator. We'll be back in Manaus before they can go anywhere."

"The first thing I want to do is celebrate. There for a while I didn't think I'd ever see Manaus again."

"One celebration coming up tonight."

This time going over the sea of green Samantha didn't feel so frightened. They had brushed death and survived. She knew from the two men that Mark was still alive. Somehow she would find her brother and everything would be fine.

Her smile was full of satisfaction when the plane began to sputter. Alarmed, Samantha sat up in her seat and looked at Brock. "What's wrong?"

Brock examined the instrument panel. "We've just run out of gas."

"Gas?" She knew there was a reason she didn't like to fly.

"Yeah, the stuff that makes this little baby go."

"Tell me you're kidding."

The engine died and they started to descend.

"Afraid not," Brock replied, his gaze searching the quickly approaching terrain below.

CHAPTER SEVEN

Stunned, Samantha tensed, bracing her hands in front of her for the collision. Her gaze was riveted to the green carpet of trees below; her mind went blank.

As the plane glided quickly downward on the air currents, Brock looked for a place to land. But they were flying over dense jungle with no clearings. In the distance he spied a river and realized that it was their only hope of survival. He maneuvered the plane toward the narrow strip of water and hoped they could stay up long enough to clear the high trees along its bank.

The jungle kept getting closer, looking like a ravenous monster ready to devour them. Suddenly Samantha couldn't look any longer. She squeezed her eyes closed and almost laughed when she remembered she hadn't paid one of her book distributors before she left New Orleans.

The jarring impact pitched Samantha forward, her head smashing into the panel; then she was thrown back in the seat. For a few seconds blackness hovered. She felt dizzy, her skull pounding from a bump on her forehead, but she was alive. They hadn't actually crashed, she realized. *Brock actually landed this thing!*

She slowly straightened, amazed that her body even worked. Opening her eyes, she expected to see green trees surrounding them. But instead, the plane was in the middle of a river and was being carried downstream on its current. They were sitting at an angle, one wing partially below the water.

Brock!

Samantha's gaze veered to him. He was slumped forward, his body seemingly lifeless, his head against the wheel, his eyes closed. Blood from a long cut on his forehead ran down his face. The sight of his wound galvanized Samantha into action. With a trembling hand she felt on his neck until she found his pulse. To Samantha's immense relief it was steady and strong.

Taking a tissue from her canvas bag, she wiped the blood from his wound and face. She was thankful that the blood was already starting to clot. Past bandaging and cleaning a wound, she didn't know what she was supposed to do for an accident victim.

She was considering tearing her extra cotton

blouse to use as a bandage when she remembered the first aid kit Brock had put under her seat before they left Manaus. From the kit she withdrew the necessary items to cleanse and bandage his gash. She dabbed a cotton swab soaked with antiseptic on his wound, tentatively at first, but when she realized she wasn't getting anywhere, she used more pressure.

Coming to, Brock moaned, batting her hand away. "Remind me never to leave a wake-up call with you, lady," he mumbled, touching his forehead and wincing.

Samantha continued to clean his wound, ignoring his glares. "The nurses must love seeing you come into a hospital."

"I wouldn't know. Never had the pleasure."

Samantha smoothed a bandage over his cut, aware of how glad she was that he was sitting next to her, even if he was complaining. His voice sounded wonderful.

As Brock perused the interior of the plane, he saw the cut on her leg that had ripped her pants. "Turnabout is fair play, Sam."

The mischief in his eyes made her wary of his intent. She tightened the hold on the bottle of antiseptic.

Grinning, he took the bottle from her tight grasp and began to administer his own special kind of first aid. His touch was gentle but efficient. Before she had time to catch her breath, she had a bandage on her own wound.

The more she was around him the more she was discovering how full of contradictions Brock Slader was. He could be so incredibly gentle, and yet full of strength and power at the same time.

"Though I would love to stay here all day and chat, we've got to get out of here." Brock continued his visual inventory of the interior of the plane.

"How? You forgot to fill up back in Manaus. And I doubt we'll float by a gas station."

"There was enough gas to get us to the mission and back. That's something I always double-check. A bullet must have hit the tank when they were firing at us back there."

The plane jolted, the wing sinking farther under the water. Samantha's gaze widened as she stared out her window. The river was only a few feet from her door.

"This plane isn't going to stay afloat much longer. There's a rubber raft in the back that we'll use. The friend I borrowed this from always has certain provisions in case of a wreck."

"A wreck! You thought we might wreck and you didn't tell me?"

"No, I didn't think we would. But it does happen, and this is no place to be caught without certain necessities. It's a precaution that can make the difference between life and death. Parts of the Amazon are still unexplored."

"Are we in one of those parts?" She tried to keep her voice steady. This was not what she had had in mind when she had come to Brazil to find her brother.

"No, but as you can see it isn't a main thoroughfare. I'll set up the raft while you gather up everything you think we'll need. We don't have much time." Brock was already reaching into the storage area in back of his seat for the raft.

The plane shifted again, and Samantha was afraid to move too suddenly. She gingerly picked up her canvas tote and Brock's backpack, then stuffed the first aid kit into her bag.

Brock handed her two bundles from the back, saying, "We'll need these hammocks. Hold on to them and stay in here while I get the raft set up. Then come out on the wing when I tell you with as little movement as possible."

"What if . . ." Her voice trailed off into silence. Brock was already opening his door and climbing out of the cockpit. What if the water started coming in while she was still in here? she finished silently as she watched Brock inflate the raft.

Samantha glanced out her window at the water, now only a foot from her door, and decided to scoot to the far side where Brock had been. When the raft was fully blown up, Brock, holding it to the side of the plane, motioned for Samantha to get into the raft.

She crept out of the cockpit, keeping her gaze diverted from the river. After throwing the bags and hammocks into the bottom, she started to slide down the plane's side inch by slow inch into the raft. Being so close to the water brought back all her fears of drowning and her father's death. She was almost ready to take her chances with the plane when it lurched once again, and water gushed into the cockpit she had just left.

"No time for grace." Brock pushed Samantha the rest of the way and quickly followed.

The raft swayed under their jolting weight and water poured over one side, leaving an inch of water in the raft's bottom. Samantha, panic stricken, clutched at the sides to steady herself and the raft.

With an oar Brock shoved them away from the sinking plane. While the raft was caught in the river's current and moving away from the plane, the aircraft went under, but the tip of one wing remained protruding out of the water.

"Damn! I was hoping nothing would be left showing," Brock muttered as he began to steer the raft in the current.

"Why? This way we can find the plane and maybe salvage it." She wondered who would have to pay for the damage. She wouldn't be able to take a vacation for a decade at this rate. How much did a plane cost? she wondered.

"If we can find it, so can the bogus padres."

"You said they wouldn't be going anywhere for the next day or so. We'll be safe—"

"Sam, if we're lucky, we'll be celebrating our escape in Manaus this time next week."

"A week! It only took us a few hours to get to the mission."

"A straight shot over some rough terrain." He gave her a quick, reassuring smile, then continued to navigate the raft downstream. "I suggest you put on that hat you bought. It's going to be a long, hot day. Then you might try and do something about the water in the bottom of the raft before it soaks everything."

After donning the hat, Samantha looked from one bank of the river, with its wall of trees and overhanging branches, to the other side, an exact replica. Seven days of this? She couldn't believe her misfortune. Green wasn't even her favorite color.

Rolling up the long sleeves of her blouse because it was so hot, she spent the next thirty minutes bailing water out of the raft with a collapsible travel cup she had in her tote. She placed their bags on top of the hammocks so their things wouldn't get wet. It wouldn't be long in this heat before the little water left in the raft evaporated. Tired from the small amount of exertion, Samantha sat back to examine in detail the terrain they were passing through.

For a long time they traveled in silence, the only sounds those of nature, but there were many of those. Samantha gave up counting how many different kinds of birds were along the river or taking flight overhead. Every once in a while she would hear a shrill or a roar and wonder what creature could possibly have made that sound. She never wanted to come face to face with whatever they were.

After an hour of watching the same monotonous, peaceful scenery, Samantha longed for the frantic pace of her life in New Orleans. Never again would she wish to do nothing but sit and vegetate.

She had purposely avoided looking at Brock as he sat in the front of the raft. He stirred feelings in her she didn't want to feel. The muscles in his arms and back rippled with each stroke of the oar, the skin on the nape of his neck glistening with sweat. He was in superb physical shape, but he wasn't her ideal man. At least, she didn't think he was; to be honest, she still didn't know that much about him.

She looked away from his broad back, his shirt pulled enticingly across it. It seemed they would be stuck together for the next week. She certainly couldn't spend the time fantasizing about him. She was a sensible woman who didn't do unrealistic things, and getting involved with a man like Brock Slader was definitely unrealistic. They had nothing in common short of being members of the human race.

Her attention was pulled away from the man in front of her by a prickling sensation on her hands and arms. There was a reddish hue to her skin that rivaled her hair in color, and she suddenly realized the folly of rolling up her sleeves. Yesterday—was it only yesterday that they were safe in Manaus?—Brock had insisted that she buy sunscreen as well as the straw hat. She delved into her canvas bag for the lotion, but her fingers clasped her brother's black book first.

Taking it out, she looked through it, puzzled by what Mark had told her over the phone. This book somehow contained something of great value. What? The pages were written in letters and numbers, none of which made sense in English.

She studied one series of coded words. The sequence seemed familiar, but like a dream a person forgets when he awakens in the morning, what seemed familiar was just out of reach of her memory. The dull throbbing in her head from the bump increased even more from the heat and mental exhaustion.

Samantha decided to find a safer place to put the book until she could inspect it more closely. She emptied out her waterproof makeup bag and placed the book in it. After the raft had almost tipped over earlier, she didn't want to take any chances.

After securing the book in the safest place that she could think of and then tying her bag to the raft, Samantha lavished sunscreen on her arms and face, a white film now covering her skin. "Would you like some sunscreen?" she asked Brock.

"Don't need it." He tossed his reply over his shoulder but never turned toward her. Neither did his even paddling rhythm stop.

How could someone be so comfortable with silence? Samantha wondered, exasperated that he hadn't said more, something to open up the conversation for her.

Left to her own devices again, Samantha began to go over in her mind the events of the last twenty-four hours. A disturbing question surfaced immediately. How did Carlos and Paul know she was going to be at the Para Mission? They had been waiting for her, and the only other person who knew she was going to the mission was Brock.

Doubt about him began to nag at Samantha. She really knew very little about him short of his name and that he was from Houston, with a father and sister still alive. Any or all of what he had told her could be a lie.

What if he had been waiting for her in the lobby of the Grand Hotel? What if he had intended all along to "help" her search for Mark because he wanted to find her brother as badly as she did? What if his act in Manaus had been carefully orchestrated from the very beginning to gain her confidence? What if he was working for himself and in her saw an opportunity to make a lot of money—more than his ten percent? Her temples pounded painfully with her doubts and questions.

She had to discover who Brock Slader really was and what he was doing in the Amazon, thousands of miles from Houston, Texas. Then maybe she would be able to tell if she could really trust him or if he was working with Carlos and Paul, or just for himself. Even in the grueling heat of the noon day sun, she shivered. Though perspiration beaded her forehead, she was chilled by the knowledge she couldn't trust anyone, not even Brock.

When Brock started to paddle toward the shore, Samantha wondered if Carlos and Paul would be waiting for her in the thicket of the trees. Every shadow took on a menacing shape in her mind as the raft neared a stretch of sandy beach.

"Why are we stopping?"

Brock jumped onto the shore and dragged the raft onto the beach with Samantha still in it, clinging to the sides. "It's not wise to travel in the hottest part of the day. We'll rest for a few hours."

Was Brock waiting for an accomplice to catch up with them? "I'd rather continue and put more distance between us and them."

"There is a very good reason why people in the tropics take siestas. The heat, Sam. It saps all your strength. And since I'm steering, I'm resting." Without waiting for her he took the hammocks out of the raft and began to string them up. When he had completed his task, he faced her. "I suggest you do the same. It's going to be a hard week."

She remained in the raft, staring at him, so strong, so capable of crushing her. Could he be such an accomplished actor? Could he be the one after her brother? The doubts and questions swirled in her mind and she didn't move.

"Suit yourself," he said with a shrug, and lay down in one of the hammocks in the shade of the tropical rain forest.

The hot sun beat down on Samantha unmercifully. The beads of perspiration became rivulets of sweat that quickly soaked her clothing. Her straw hat did little to relieve the heat, especially now that there wasn't even a hot breeze created by the raft's movement. Her eyelids began to drift closed. Drowsiness crept over her like a heavy fog. Her body slumped forward.

A macaw shrieked.

Samantha jerked back upright. She had to stay awake. But she looked longingly at the empty hammock, then at Brock, asleep in his. She could count the hours of sleep that she had had in the last two nights on one hand. Maybe she could just lie down and at least rest her eyes for a little while. She could be up and back in the raft before Brock.

Tiptoeing past Brock's hammock, she paused, drawn to the innocent expression on his face while he was sleeping. A lock of black hair had fallen across his forehead, and Samantha was tempted to smooth it back. Alarmed that she could so easily be taken in by his serene features, she stepped away and hurried toward her hammock before she gave the man her brother's book on a silver platter.

She clutched her bag to her chest and settled into the hammock, determined to be alert and cautious around Brock Slader. But five minutes after she lay down on the canvas bed, which cradled her like a warm cocoon, she was asleep, the hammock's gentle rocking motion lulling her into a state of languor. . . .

In the early-morning mist Brock and she cut through the vines and trees, their movements rushed. The shouts of the pursuers were getting nearer, and with each step they took the foliage was thicker and harder to get through. When she and Brock burst out of the dense jungle onto a cliff overlooking a waterfall, they stared at each other then back behind them. The shouts grew louder.

Suddenly Carlos and Paul emerged from the jungle, their guns aimed at her, smiles of immense satisfaction on their faces. Carlos motioned with his gun for Brock to move away from her, leaving her to face the three of them. They advanced on her; she took a step back, then another, until her foot was at the edge of the cliff.

"We want the book," Brock demanded. "You can't escape us now."

She clutched her bag to her chest and shook her head. "Never!"

Brock's hand snaked out and circled her wrist, yanking her to him with a wrenching jolt. She fought the power of his grip, her nails digging into his flesh. . . .

"Ouch! Sam, my God, wake up!"

Her eyelids flew open and Brock stood over her, her hand in a death grip on his arm. Her throat was parched, robbing her of speech.

"What did you dream this time? Jumping into a hole full of snakes?"

With his knowledge of her fears, like snakes and water, he could extract anything from her. In that moment she realized just how vulnerable she was—if Brock was working for Carlos and Paul or for himself and against her. She had to find out before her vivid imagination conjured up all kinds of things, none very appealing.

She eased her fingers open and snatched her

hand away from him. "I wasn't dreaming about the Amazon," she lied. "It was about Mardi Gras. Some of those costumes can be frightening." She sat up and swung her legs over the hammock's edge, continuing to chatter to give herself time to settle down. "But even so, Mardi Gras is still one of my favorite times of the year. I hate missing it, but the way things are going, I won't get back in time."

"We should be back in Manaus in time for the celebration there. Brazil goes all out for the Carnival season, especially Rio."

Samantha's stomach rumbled with hunger. "I hate to ask this, but is there anything to eat in the jungle?"

"Yes, but we don't have time now. I want to put more distance between us and the plane while it's still light."

Her stomach protested again as she stood and began to take down her hammock, following Brock's instructions.

"You seem to have everything else in that bag of yours. Do you have anything to eat until we stop for the night?" Brock asked.

"I thought you were the one who was always prepared."

"There is a limit," he said wryly.

As they walked to the raft, in her mind Samantha went over the contents of her tote bag and suddenly remembered the peanuts that she hadn't eaten on the flight to Brazil. Within seconds she had the two bags of peanuts in her hand.

"Do you happen to have a bottle of beer in that bag of yours?"

"Sorry, there is a limit," Samantha retorted as she handed him his peanuts.

As they ate, Samantha wondered if she was feeding the enemy. But so what? He was her ticket out of the jungle, like it or not. She was completely at his mercy, and they both knew it.

Back on the river again, Samantha decided to see what she could discover about Brock Slader. "When was the last time you saw your sister?"

"A while back. Why?"

"No reason. I know some people in Houston. Maybe we have a friend in common. Who are some people you know?"

"I doubt we know the same people. Houston is a big place."

"Have you met any other Americans in Manaus?"

"One or two."

So much for subtlety, Samantha thought. "Why are you in the Amazon?"

Brock's spine stiffened. He stopped paddling and tilted his head.

Puzzled, Samantha asked another question. "Why did you really go with me to the Para Mission?"

Brock hurriedly began to paddle toward the shaded bank.

Samantha stared at their destination. There wasn't anyplace to land the raft along the shore. "What are you doing? Answer me!"

"I hear a plane."

CHAPTER EIGHT

The bush plane flew low along the river, as though whoever was in it was looking for something—or someone. Samantha and Brock held on to an overhanging branch of a tree to keep the raft from drifting out of their hiding place.

As the sound of the plane faded in the distance, Brock looped a rope around a branch to secure the raft. "You can let go now. We'll wait awhile before moving on."

Her fingers held the bark as if they were frozen in place. Normal people weren't supposed to be scared for their lives like this, she thought, and started to pry her fingers loose.

"Don't move, Sam," Brock whispered furiously.

"Make up your mind!" she protested. Then she felt something slide over her hand. Her gaze swerved to the branch above her head. A two-foot, brown-patterned snake was slithering along the branch and across her fingers. She was paralyzed with fear, and yet mesmerized, too, by the almost lazy way the snake moved.

Brock slowly eased his machete from the sheath at his side and when the snake's head was past Samantha's hand, he sprang forward, striking the reptile behind its head.

The snake's severed head dropped onto the bottom of the raft; the body landed in Samantha's lap. As though in a trance she released her grip on the branch and brought both her arms close to her chest. Shocked, she stared down at the snake in her lap.

"Sam?"

Concern laced Brock's voice as he lifted the snake off her lap and threw it into the water, along with its head. A moment later the river churned with ferocious action, as though the water were boiling. Still dazed, Samantha looked from her lap to the water where the snake had been. Then she turned her wide gaze on Brock.

"Piranhas," Brock replied to the silent question in her eyes.

"What kind of snake was that?" she asked, her voice a weak thread.

He glanced away, the river suddenly absorbing his full attention.

"What kind, Brock?"

"A fer-de-lance."

"Oh, my God." Her eyelids slid closed, and she took in one deep breath after another. One of the deadliest snakes in the world had just slithered over her hand. If it weren't for Brock, she would be dead now.

Then Brock was beside her, his arm slipping around her to pull her close.

"This place isn't for a novice, Sam. The life-and-death struggle in the jungle is too intense. A deadly predator is eaten by a deadly predator."

Her life in New Orleans had been very sheltered, she realized. She had lived in a world of books and had read about many places and subjects, but had never really comprehended the struggles for existence that went on in other parts of the world. When—*if*—she ever returned to the United States, she would never take the luxuries of life for granted again.

"Life in the jungle is surviving one day to the next." His arm tightened about her. "Are you all right now?"

"Yes, I think so." She leaned away and looked into his silver-gray eyes. "One good thing came out of this incident. After that close encounter I think I just took a crash course in how to lose your fear of snakes." Her laugh was shaky, but she managed to smile.

He laughed, too, a warm, delicious sound that drowned out all the other jungle noises. Framing her face with his large, powerful hands, he drew her to him, his lips brushing across hers in a fleeting kiss that quickly evolved into more. Breaths tangled; tongues dueled.

His caressing fingers glided to the curve of her neck, holding her still as his tongue licked the corners of her mouth. With tiny grazes of his lips he trailed a path to her earlobe and bit down lovingly on its shell.

Samantha wanted to surrender to the excruciating sensations he generated in her. But her silent war raged. Was Brock Slader her savior or her jailer? With the sobering question came reality. She pulled away, wedging her arms between them.

"I'm fine now. Don't you think we ought to be on our way?" She met the desire in his eyes with an unwavering directness. She couldn't give in to the part of her that wanted him as Eve had wanted Adam in the first garden paradise.

He said nothing, but untied the rope and pushed off.

While he steered the raft back out into the current, Samantha was able to compose her traitorous emotions. She wouldn't allow that to happen again, she vowed. They still had seven days to go, but she was a strong-willed person.

Yet as she watched him paddle, she was struck by his earthy masculinity. He fit in with the wilderness because there was an element of untamed primitiveness in him. He was at ease with nature at its core, its raw essence. He reminded her of an early explorer of the Americas who could be at home in a dugout canoe, going where no one else had been, or at court among the lords and ladies.

As they headed down the river, they kept close to the shaded bank. The silence between them, broken only by the sound of rain falling from time to time, stretched out like the river in front of them.

Finally Samantha decided she didn't want a repeat of the morning's silence. "Who do you think was in the plane?"

"Could be anybody."

"Carlos and Paul?"

"Very likely."

"How did they get a plane?"

"Called in reinforcements, probably." The even rhythm of his paddling continued, splash, lift, splash. "Whoever's after your brother is now definitely after us. They think we know something. We can't trust anyone, Sam. This operation might be bigger than we thought. It's obvious they'll go to great lengths to get their hands on what they think we have."

Can't trust anyone. Samantha was afraid she couldn't trust Brock even after he had saved her life. Carlos and Paul had been waiting for her at the mission. How had they known? The only answer she could come up with was that Brock told them that morning he went out to make his calls. Had Carlos and Paul betrayed him at the mission for some reason?

Now, she had to wonder if he even called the hospitals. Maybe Mark was injured or ill and in one of them.

She felt betrayed, and yet there was a part of her that didn't think Brock was capable of that kind of treachery. He could have simply let the fer-de-lance bite her if he wanted to be rid of her—unless for some reason they wanted her alive. As miles of endless jungle passed, her doubts mushroomed and her nerves tautened like a band pulled to its limit. It was only a matter of time before they snapped from the tension.

"I've never seen so many animals in one place, not even in the zoo in New Orleans. A zoologist would be in heaven here." And she would trade places in a second's notice with any zoologists in the world, Samantha added silently as she stared at Brock's back.

"For that matter, a botanist could spend his whole life categorizing plants and still not get to all of them. I think I have a few smaller versions of some of these same plants back home. And the minute I return home I'm going to throw out all my houseplants. I never want to be surrounded by so much greenery again. I think I've seen every imaginable shade of the color that there is and probably a few I didn't know existed."

One part of her listened to her prattle and wondered when Brock, a man of few words, would jump overboard to get away. The other part of her couldn't seem to stop the unnecessary babble as a way to disguise her extreme nervousness.

"When I get home, the first thing I'm going to do is eat a big New Orleans feast at the best restaurant in the French Quarter. No, first—after I deplant my house—I guess I'll soak in a hot tub of scented water for a good hour, then I'll dress up and go out to eat with a crowd of at least twenty friends. What will you do?"

"I won't be returning to the States."

"Where will you go?"

He shrugged, not once looking back at her.

"Well, then I'll curl up in my bed." She hesitated, realizing her nervous chattering was leading her into dangerous territory.

"And what will you do in bed?"

Hearing the amusement in Brock's voice, she glared at his back. "Read all the books that I've missed since I was gone."

"That many."

"When was the last time you read a book?" she asked defensively.

"I read one a few years back."

"Oh, that many." To Samantha, who loved books, it was a crime that a person didn't read more than one every three years.

Brock laughed, the sound angering her even more. Nothing bothered him!

"I'd rather experience life than read about it, Sam. I haven't found myself bored enough to sit down and read."

"Bored! My life isn't boring. I read because I enjoy it. It transports me to places I've never been. I learn about things I would never have an opportunity to firsthand."

"I like to go to those places. I like to do those things firsthand. If you want to bad enough, you can find a way."

"Some people have to stay home and run things. If everyone dropped everything and traveled all over the world having adventures or whatever you have, who would keep things going?"

"There are always people who are too afraid to do what they really want to in their heart."

"First you call me bored and now you call me afraid." Her anger was mounting and surpassing her wariness.

"You're the only one who can be the judge of what you're truly feeling."

So now she had a philosophic adventurer as a traveling companion. "Do you advocate that I sell my bookstore and travel to those places I read about?"

The oar sliced into the water ten times before he finally answered, "No. I can't picture you letting yourself go and taking each thing that happens to you as it comes. You have to have things neat and orderly, everything planned. As you can see, life in the jungle isn't something you can plan."

She was disconcerted that he had read her so well. She couldn't picture herself letting herself go and taking things as they happened either.

"I suppose that's one of the reasons there are books," Brock continued. "I agree with you that everyone can't go or do everything."

"Well, I'm one person who's extremely glad there is a need for books. If not, I would go out of business." If they were at such opposite poles on this issue, Samantha could just imagine how they stood on other subjects.

"Don't get me wrong. I think there's a definite place for books in this world."

"Where? The library or someone's closet?"

"No, I think more like a fireplace. Books are made from trees. Great for burning," he teased, laughter edging his voice.

A comedian as well as a philosopher, she thought. She'd be entertained, saved, and philosophized all at the same time. What an exciting week!

In the next stretch of the river there were a lot more sandbars to negotiate. Brock fell silent, his concentration on the water ahead of the raft. Ten minutes into the silence Samantha realized just how much she had enjoyed

136

their verbal exchange, even if they didn't believe in any of the same things.

Samantha was contemplating how to start a new conversation when she heard the roar. Alert, she sat up and listened. The roar grew closer as Brock paddled. She had a sinking feeling she knew what was ahead of them—between her and Manaus.

"What's that?" she asked, praying Brock wouldn't confirm what she thought.

"A waterfall."

Flashes from her nightmare inundated her.

"We'll stop there for the night. Tomorrow morning we'll portage around it. There's nothing to worry about, Sam."

"Great! How many more of these do we have to portage around?"

"I'm not sure. Three at least."

As they neared the waterfall, Brock angled the raft toward the shore, the current near the falls pulling them along faster. Samantha had visions of the raft getting caught and plunging over the waterfall. A cold sweat broke out on her forehead as she became mesmerized by the drop a few hundred yards ahead.

She was so absorbed in the waterfall that she didn't realize Brock was tying the raft to a log protruding out in the river until he clasped her arm to get her attention. She scrambled to the front and he helped her step onto the log; then she walked the few feet to the bank. As he unloaded the raft, he handed the items to her and she placed their meager belongings in a pile by her feet.

When Brock hoisted the empty raft up and over his head, Samantha was amazed at his sense of balance as he tightroped along the log to shore. Putting the raft down by their belongings, he took his machete from its sheath and began to hack the vines in front of him.

"What are you doing?" she asked, watching the movement of his muscles as his blade attacked the foliage, more interested in them than his answer.

"Finding us a place to make camp for the night."

A short distance into the jungle there was a clearing where Brock set up camp and slung the hammocks.

"While I'm gone, start a fire," he commanded, picking up his gun.

"Gone? Where are you going?" She would take back all the negative things she thought about him not to be left alone.

"Grocery shopping."

"May I come too?"

"We need a fire. It will be dark soon. Besides, Sam, I'll move faster without you tagging along."

She wasn't a dog, she fumed silently, determined to show him she could do something

138

worthwhile. She wasn't totally dependent on him.

While Brock scouted for food, Samantha gathered wood, not going more than a foot from the clearing, and began the fire. When she stepped back to survey her work, pleased with her contribution, she collided with a solid wall of muscles and warmth—human warmth. With her nightmare at the waterfall in mind, she spun about with her hands clenched ready to defend herself. She found Brock standing behind her with a wide grin on his face.

"Next time you sneak up on someone, whistle," she said breathlessly.

"Sorry. A habit of mine."

His grin was sheer sexiness, and Samantha had to look away. "What are you, a soldier of fortune?" The question had come out before she realized what she was saying, but now she wanted to know the real answer. Had Carlos and Paul hired Brock to take care of her, then decided to do the job themselves? Or had Brock decided he wanted one hundred percent of whatever her brother had found? Was he working for himself or someone else? Did she have something to fear from him?

"We're in luck. I found some pyxidiums that contain Brazil nuts." He held up two balls, each the size of a grapefruit. "We'll roast them over the fire, then I'll open them. I also found some water to drink."

"Water? With all that?" Samantha gestured toward the river.

"This is better. Less likely to make you sick, even though this river water is okay."

"Where's the water? All you've got is a stick."

He cut a section of the vine and held it over his mouth. Water began to drip from the vine. He passed it to Samantha, who was astonished at just how thirsty she was. It was the best thing she had tasted.

"And for dessert I have some yellow *okwashik* berries. They're like hard orange candy."

Samantha was starved and the Brazil nuts were delicious, having a moist white meat better than a coconut's. Even the "dessert" was good, and by the time she had finished eating, she felt sated.

"Tomorrow night we'll stop earlier. I want to go farther and get some meat. If we're lucky tomorrow we might find some turtles along the way."

"I used to have two pet turtles named Fred and Susie. I don't know if I could eat one."

He pinned her with a penetrating gaze, the hunter in him evident. "Sam, if it means your survival, you will. Contrary to food shopping in the States, in the jungle you don't always have a wide variety or even a choice of what to eat.

You take what nature gives you and you're damn grateful for it."

Samantha rose and dusted off her pants. Looking at him with an equally piercing gaze, she said, "You've purposely avoided my questions about what you do for a living. You won't tell me why you refused to be my guide and then suddenly accepted the job of taking me to the mission. Why, Brock? I want an answer, and changing the subject won't work this time."

He stood, gaining the height advantage. "For money. What other reason is there?"

"What do you need the money for?"

"Some things aren't your business." He pivoted and strode from the clearing, disappearing into the jungle as if the trees and vines had swallowed him up.

It left her utterly alone. Suddenly the sounds of the jungle, that she had begun to take for granted, were magnified, and the dark shadows of the approaching night were growing. Looking around, Samantha thought of the time when she was eight and had stayed up all night to overcome her fear of the dark. Her mind had visualized all kinds of monsters in the shadows, waiting for her to fall asleep. But before morning had come, she had faced the fear and had won. Never again had the dark bothered her.

The memory prompted her to try and come

to terms with her nightmare of the waterfall. She made her way to it, pushing away plants and lianas from her path. At the falls she saw the sun begin to set, the horizon a blood red. Then she gazed down into the churning water at the bottom. There was a raw beauty about the scene that turned Samantha's fear into appreciation.

The lure of nature was strong, and Samantha could understand the attraction that Brock had for the jungle. While she realized she belonged back in civilization, she felt that Brock was probably more comfortable here, in a place that reminded her of the beginning of time. Man did not control the land; the land dominated, often reclaiming what man had taken.

Samantha was mesmerized by the power and deafening sound of the waterfall. She hadn't realized how quickly it grew dark at the equator, but in five minutes the sun had set and the black shadows engulfed her.

When a hand settled heavily on her shoulder, she gasped, jerking away from the touch. Her foot slipped at the edge of the waterfall, and she felt herself falling. Her arms flung outward; she latched onto a hand and held on to the warm flesh.

Brock caught her and easily lifted her to her feet. She collapsed against him, clinging to him for a moment as she got a decent breath. All she could hear was the waterfall; all she could see was a faint outline of Brock, but she felt safe again in his arms.

When her pulse began to slow, she tilted back her head to look at Brock. He placed his thumb under her chin and bent his head toward hers. His other hand moved down her spine, spanned her buttocks, and pulled her even closer. Pressed flat against him, she felt the tremendous pounding of his heart, his firm muscles, his warm breath on her cheek.

Her arms found their way around his neck, and she was the one who urged his mouth to hers. Her tongue slipped in between his slightly parted lips and slid over the smoothness of his teeth. Their kiss became as raw as the waterfall behind them, their passion as intense as the struggle for survival in this primitive environment.

His fingers pulled the pins from her hair and wove through its lush richness, holding her head still as his mouth ravished hers again and again. When his tongue dipped inside her mouth, their breath and tastes merged, forming a potent combination that was headier than a rich wine. It intoxicated her senses and made her feel drunk with her aching need.

Then his hand drifted lower, past the curve of her neck to the swell of her breasts. His fingers worked the buttons loose on her blouse and pushed the material aside. Slipping inside her bra, he cupped one breast in his large hand

and squeezed gently. The touch of his flesh against hers was like liquid fire, melting their bodies together.

Her head fell back in wonder, and he nuzzled the hollow at the base of her throat, then nibbled a tingling path down until his teeth enclosed her hardened nipple. He suckled her breast, sending hot currents of pleasure through her trembling body.

Her fingernails dug into his shoulders as a moan escaped her lips. "Please, Brock."

When he lifted his head, his silver eyes were full of longing and passion. Time seemed to become suspended. Then suddenly they came together, kissing, embracing, and Samantha became lost in the fevered interplay of their bodies.

Brock swept her up into his arms and carried her toward their camp. Placing her gently into the hammock, the glow of the fire reflecting their passion-shrouded expressions, he paid homage to her beauty, her hair fanning across the canvas like a wild flame. Her eyes, the color of brandy, were heavy with desire. Her chest rose and fell rapidly with her labored breathing, the enticing swell of her breasts arousing him even more.

He should walk away now before it was too late, he thought, but he couldn't. She was like a rare orchid high in a tree, unattainable to all but the daring. He would curse himself in the morning, because making love to her would complicate an already difficult situation, but he wanted the orchid for his own.

He couldn't resist the sensual appeal in her eyes. With no regard to the consequences, he found himself reaching down to trail his fingers along her neck to the valley between her breasts.

"Sam"—her name was torn from his lips as he leaned over to kiss her.

Samantha stiffened. Hearing Brock call her Sam doused the fire that raged inside. It reminded her of the reason she was in the jungle with him: her brother's disappearance. It reminded her of the questions about Brock that she had to have answers to.

Brock straightened, seeing immediately the change in Samantha. It cooled his desire and put his emotions in perspective. One part of him was thankful; the other was unfulfilled, dissatisfied.

Samantha fumbled with the buttons of her blouse as she swung her legs over the edge of the hammock. "Why do you need the money, Brock?"

He walked to the fire and sat on his haunches, staring into the flames as he rubbed the back of his neck. Indecision was apparent in his usually closed expression. Samantha moved to the circle of fire but remained standing a few feet from him, perched like a bird, ready to take flight if danger was evident.

"I don't answer to anyone and haven't for a long time. I've made a point to keep it that way."

"Please. I need to know." She hated the desperation in her voice, but she didn't want to spend the next seven days wondering if she could trust him.

"I need the money for an oil deal. I'm an independent geologist. I have to have twenty-five thousand dollars if I want a quarter interest in a project I've been putting together in the Amazon. Of course, my services are included as part of my share." He thought of the Latin he had been doing business with; Brock wished he could finance the whole deal.

"A geologist! I thought you might be—"

His robust laugh cut off the rest of her statement. "You thought I was an uneducated bum, a soldier of fortune, or someone like that."

She blushed and looked down at her feet. "Well, your opinion of books, staying at the Grand Hotel, having lived in the jungle . . ."

"All add up to an unsavory character?" One eyebrow rose mockingly.

She couldn't meet his steadfast gaze. "Actually, a lot worse. How did Carlos and Paul know we were going to be at the mission?"

He frowned, thought a moment, and replied, "Paul was in your room. Perhaps he

146

bugged it. Or when we were in the lobby checking out of the Grand Hotel, maybe one of us mentioned the Para Mission and someone overheard us. Why do you ask?"

"I thought you were working for Carlos and Paul and that you had told them. You're always so damn mysterious."

She braced herself for his anger, but was surprised when Brock threw back his head and laughed again, a rich, deep sound.

"No wonder you've been giving me frightful glances all day."

"Not all day," she protested, realizing she might have misjudged him.

"No, not when we were kissing." His voice mellowed and his eyes clouded with a sensuality that was almost palpable.

Flustered by the way he could make her forget everything sensible, she asked the first thing that came to mind. "What's a geologist doing in the jungle?"

One corner of his mouth quirked. "Looking for oil."

"The Amazon has a lot?"

"We're just scratching the surface, so to speak. But the potential is there."

"Why here?"

"Why not here?" He lifted his shoulder in a shrug as if to say it was a natural place for him to look.

"Oh, I don't know. You have to battle so much just to get where you're going."

"I like the challenge."

"Ah, yes. That's why you agreed to take me to the mission—that and the hope of a treasure."

He rose to his feet and stretched in one fluid movement, the gesture a startlingly sexy one. "We have a lot of ground to cover tomorrow. We'd better turn in for the night, Sam."

Samantha still had a long list of questions to ask him, but she sensed his barriers, usually erected about his personal life, rising back into place. Tomorrow she would delve a little deeper and find out why he preferred the jungle to living in Houston. Personally, she couldn't imagine anyone voluntarily choosing the Amazon over a city in the States—or anywhere for that matter.

She had started to walk past him to her hammock when he reached for her wrist and stopped her. She stared into his gleaming gray eyes and had to fight the urge to throw herself against him. No man had a right to be so full of masculine vitality.

He raised his hand to cup her face. "I wouldn't hurt you, Sam. You have nothing to fear from me." Then, almost reluctantly, he dropped his hand to his side and made his way to his hammock.

She was beginning to believe she had nothing to fear from Brock, but she wasn't so sure about herself. She was changing since she had come to the Amazon, and the new aspects of her personality confused her. In her hammock she tried to sleep, but the strangeness of being in the middle of a jungle out in the open kept her awake for hours. And when she finally fell asleep, her dreams were riddled with images of herself and Brock, embracing, kissing, making love.

She woke with a start, her eyes opening quickly. Standing over her were five Indians, painted red and black with lips discs in their mouths and feathered plugs in their noses and earlobes. Her gaze flew to Brock's hammock. It was empty. Then she looked back at the Indian nearest her. He was holding a six-foot bow with an arrow strung and aimed at her. Tied around his waist was a shrunken head.

The Indian lowered the bow and arrow and reached toward Samantha's head. She tried to scream, but nothing would come out.

CHAPTER NINE

The Indian with the shrunken head touched Samantha's hair and said something to his companions. They all nodded in total agreement with whatever he had said. Her scalp tingled as her thoughts raced with possibilities of what the leader had said; none of them were very inviting.

The Indian again reached out toward her. Finally she screamed, a bloodcurdling sound that sent all five Indians jumping back, confusion on their faces.

An eternity passed as Samantha stared wide eyed at the Indians and they looked at each other, then back at her.

Brock charged into the clearing, halted, and surveyed the six people who turned toward him. He took one look at the group of Indians, then at Samantha's pale face, and he laughed.

"If this is funny, please let me in on the joke," Samantha said between clenched teeth.

She eased out of the hammock, skirting their

five "visitors" and moving slowly toward Brock. She brushed her long unbound hair behind her shoulders and kept stepping inch by slow inch toward the fringe of the trees where Brock was.

When Samantha was halfway there, Brock moved forward, approaching the Indian who had touched her hair, and greeted him in his native language. Then he said something to each of the other four Indians. It looked like a damn class reunion, Samantha thought, her heart still pounding, as she noted the camaraderie between Brock and the Indians.

When Brock came to her side and put his arm around her shoulders, she had a sneaky suspicion he was informing them she was his "woman." The grins on all the men's faces held a wealth of meaning, and Samantha seethed at the knowing glances they exchanged.

"I may not understand the language, but I do know body language, Brock Slader, and I don't appreciate it. What did you tell them?" she whispered in a furious tone.

"That you're my—ah, friend and that we're traveling together."

His slight pause was all she needed to confirm her suspicion. "Somehow I get the impression your meaning of friend and their meaning of friend don't add up to my meaning."

"The last time I ran into them they were very friendly, but a few years back some men of the tribe did kill a scientist who had been living among them for four months."

"How can you say that so calmly?"

"I thought you had a right to know the delicacy of the situation."

"Thanks. I'd rather be ignorant."

"I don't want you to do anything you and I would regret later."

"Don't worry. Even I know a dangerous situation when I see one—or rather, all five sets of them." She looked pointedly at the bows and arrows, then at Brock, fear in her gaze. "That chief touched my hair with a gleam of ownership in his eyes."

Brock chuckled.

"Does everything amuse you? You must be one of those people who laugh in the face of death."

His expression became serious, but the glint in his eyes told Samantha it was all an act. "Sorry, Sam. The chief was just admiring your beautiful hair of fire. Perfectly innocent."

"Admiring it for what?" Her scalp still tingled, and she was sure it wasn't caused by Brock's arm about her.

"There isn't much we can do but offer them our hospitality. They want to share their kill with us."

"What kill?" She said the words louder than she had intended, and the Indians turned their attention toward her. She wished she had kept

152

quiet. It was obvious they didn't know what to make of her.

"They were hunting and killed a monkey."

"I think I'll pass."

"All I had time to gather was some fruit from a cacao tree. Monkey meat is good, especially when there isn't anything else. I don't know if I'll be able to get one. I'm a bit rusty on my hunting skills."

"How can I eat a monkey when as a child I used to love to read Curious George books?"

Muttering under his breath about picky eaters who could starve to death, Brock shook his head and walked across the clearing. While the Indians prepared the monkey meat over the fire, Brock picked up his harvest of fruit and moved back to Samantha.

Instead of giving her some cacao fruit, he handed her a cluster of orchids. "Happy Valentine's Day."

Surprised, she didn't know what to say. She stared at the delicate flowers, a touch of rare beauty in their untamed surroundings. Her throat closed as she reached out and took the cluster. Swallowing hard, she blinked to keep her tears at bay.

Samantha spun away from Brock, not wanting him to see her tears at his unexpected kindness, at his touch of gentleness in their harsh situation. Her tears rolled down her cheeks and splashed onto the orchids, and she couldn't stop them.

Silently Brock turned her toward him and drew her close against him, and she cried on his shoulder—for their predicament, for her brother, for Brock's gesture. Her tears released the tension that had been building since her brother's phone call two weeks before.

"When I swarmed the cacao tree, I found the orchids and thought you might like them," Brock whispered when her tears abated.

"Valentine's Day isn't for three days." She sniffed and he handed her his handkerchief.

"I never was one to do things when I was supposed to." He smiled, a crooked half grin that gave the impression he didn't have a care in the world.

"Now, that I believe," she said, laughing and feeling a lot better. Brock had a way of making her feel safe even amid a band of Indians who practiced shrinking heads—hopefully years ago.

The leader of the Indians said something to Brock, and he replied, then turned back to Samantha and translated, "The monkey is almost done. Are you sure you don't want to try some?"

"Absolutely." Samantha peered around Brock to look at the five Indians who were all staring at her. The chief grinned at her, revealing several missing teeth.

"Did you see what was dangling from the chief's waist?" she asked as she straightened, using Brock as a shield between herself and the Indians.

"From an enemy tribe. It's very old, but he likes to wear it as a symbol of his position. A lot of their old beliefs and practices are dying with the encroachment of civilization."

"Thank goodness! That's one practice I hope they don't suddenly decide to revive."

Brock and Samantha joined the Indians around the fire. She tried to avoid looking at the men eating the monkey meat, especially the leader with his "ornament" about his waist. All her attention was on her cacao fruit, which was tasty.

While she ate, Brock and the Indians talked. She was dying to know what they were discussing until the Indians started laughing. She looked up to find them staring at her again.

"What, or should I say who, were you talking about?"

Brock poked at the fire, adding a stick that didn't need to be added.

"You were talking about me, weren't you?"

"Yep."

When it appeared that he wasn't going to give any more details, Samantha asked, "What were you saying?" Brock Slader would be a great spy; information was extremely difficult to drag out of the man.

"The chief was giving me advice on how to handle my woman." His voice caressed the word *woman* as his eyes caressed her length.

Samantha was sure her face turned as red as her hair. "And?" She had gone this far, she might as well hear all of it.

"He said I should beat you at least once a day to keep you in line."

"Beat me!" Her gaze veered to the chief, who gave her a semitoothless grin. Thank goodness she had some sense left or she would march right over to the man and give him a piece of her mind.

"Sam."

Brock said her name with such tenderness that her attention was immediately drawn back to him.

"This tribe believes strongly in the husband's right to punish his wife physically, often cruelly. I don't condone it, but I'm not in a position to change their cultural beliefs." His voice was soft, very sober, as were his eyes as they wandered over her features.

"Those poor wives."

"As I've traveled the world, I've seen many cruel things done by one human being to another, often condoned by the society they lived in. That's a part of a 'book' I would like to skip over, but it's an integral part of the whole and not easily taken out."

She frowned. "And as you said, you aren't

156

someone who likes to rescue damsels in distress."

His eyes hardened. "I don't like to use force. There are ways to change people's beliefs quietly, subtly. I've learned the hard way that force can often backfire on you."

"What do you mean?"

"I once interfered in a fight between a husband and wife in another part of the Amazon. I ended up narrowly escaping with my life and she was exiled from the tribe. I provided for her and she lives at a mission, but she wants to live with her people. But because of me she can't. She didn't appreciate my help. The women must be reeducated as well as the men before anything can be done."

"You can't tell me women enjoy being beaten."

"No, but they don't know anything else. Remember, these tribes are very isolated and civilization is just starting to touch them."

"Thank God!"

"In the long run it will destroy the Indians and their culture if it keeps up the way it's going. Their population is quickly dwindling. Their ways, some good ones, are totally different from ours. They aren't used to our common illnesses. What we can weather often kills them. Nothing's black or white. There are always gray areas. Advancement is usually a good thing, but it might kill them."

Samantha gazed at the chief and his warriors and saw them in a different light. They knew the forest and respected it. But their ways were dying. What would their children have to face? Would the people who came to the jungle in the future understand this complex environment? Would they care as the Indians did?

When they had finished eating their breakfast, the Indians offered to help Brock and Samantha portage around the waterfall before heading back to their village. The natives moved quickly and surefootedly through the dense jungle, and Samantha had a hard time keeping up with them. Brock bridged the distance between her and the Indians.

At the bottom of the falls the Indians put the raft into the river and tied the rope to a tree trunk. Then they bade Brock and Samantha good-bye. Their appearance had disturbed her, and yet for an hour Brock and she had not been alone in the jungle. In a strange way the Indians had made the forest seem less foreign to her. They were people trying to survive in the world just like everyone else, even if she didn't agree with all their ways.

In the raft again Brock and Samantha began the long journey down the river, the miles a monotonous repetition of the day before. The sudden, occasional rainstorms forced them to the bank of the river to seek shelter under the overhanging trees. Then when the storm passed as suddenly as it appeared, they would continue as before, in silence.

Near noon Samantha decided to end the silence. "Have you always been on your own doing what you're doing now?"

"Lady, do you always ask so many personal questions?"

"I love unraveling a good mystery."

"Is there any type of book you don't like?"

"A bad one," she countered, laughing.

He continued to paddle, and she thought about pounding on his back to get his attention. Just when she'd decided that, yet again, he wasn't going to answer her, he replied, "I used to work for a large oil company in Houston. At the age of thirty I developed an ulcer. That was when I decided I wasn't cut out to work for anyone else. I love to travel, so I took off to see the world, hoping to make enough money to live on along the way."

Listening to Brock, Samantha realized he was a wanderer; she a homebody. She liked security; Brock thrived on living each day with no real regard for tomorrow, like her brother. She loved Mark, but she didn't understand him.

"Don't you worry about where your next meal will come from?"

"Nope. I always manage."

"What about your future? Retirement? IRAs?"

"For eight years I played the corporate game, and it was taking its toll on my health. I could have stayed in the game and had a heart attack at forty or I could change the way I lived. I opted for the latter. I don't worry about my future. It's useless to worry about the unknown. Wasted energy."

When the sun was almost directly overhead, they stopped for their siesta and lunch. This time there was no debate about Samantha taking a nap. She was exhausted, not having slept well for days.

Brock slung her hammock. "We'll stop early for the night. I'm going to try my hand at hunting."

He was so close that Samantha found herself reaching out and touching his arm. Part of her was shocked at her boldness; part of her was thrilled.

He laid his hand over hers and brought it to his lips, kissing each fingertip, then her palm. Gently tugging her to him, he took her mouth in a deep mating that rocked her to her very core.

When he pulled away, he whispered, "Get some sleep this time, Sam," then moved to sling his own hammock.

Frustrated, she sank down into her hammock, going over all the reasons she shouldn't fall in love with Brock Slader. The fact that he was an unemployed geologist with wanderlust in his blood was right up there.

Samantha awakened before Brock, feeling the grime and dirt of traveling. She dug into her canvas bag for her compact mirror and the makeup that she had tossed into it. There was no rule that said she couldn't at least keep up appearances as best as she could under the primitive circumstances.

She longed for a manicure and pedicure as well as a facial and shampoo. When she returned to New Orleans, she was going to treat herself to the works, she decided. But at the moment all she could do was put on some foundation, powder, and lipstick after she washed up in the river.

On the beach at the river's edge she sat on her haunches and splashed water all over her face and neck. She studied the river and thought about taking a dip to wash the sweat off her body.

"Go ahead. I think the water is okay here."

She twisted about to find Brock only a few feet behind her. "How did you know I was thinking about taking a bath?"

"Because the same thing crossed my mind, Sam. When you're roughing it, it's nice to practice a few civilized things—like a bath, a shave." Brock rubbed his hand across his several days' growth of beard.

"You know, what I'd really like to do is wash my clothes."

"You brought two shirts. Wash the one you have on and it will dry in the sun quickly."

"How? Believe it or not I didn't bring along detergent in my bag. I don't even have a bar of soap."

"Beat your clothes against those rocks over there. It's an old practice that will do for now. And if you want to wash your pants, I'll lend you my shirt to wear while you do both. It's big enough for propriety's sake."

She flashed him a smile that was both shy and appreciative. "We can afford the delay?"

"We'll take it, Sam." He squatted down beside her at the river's edge and dipped his hands into the water, then splashed it over his face and neck. "I know what a shock the jungle has been to you. And I know it hasn't been easy, so a few pleasantries are important."

"Thanks."

He turned his head to stare into her eyes. For a few moments their gazes embraced, each trying to look deep inside the other. She thought of herself as an open book, whereas Brock was a book that had to be read slowly and reread many times before a person understood everything.

A bird shrieked, breaking the hypnotic spell, and Samantha quickly stood, flustered by the feelings that Brock so easily evoked in her.

She started to walk back toward her hammock, deciding a bath and wash wouldn't be wise, when Brock called out, "I promise to keep my distance, Sam. The beach is perfect for wading into the water for a bath as well as cleaning your clothes. This may be one of the few opportunities to do either."

She sighed. "Okay."

Brock shrugged out of his white cotton shirt and offered it to Samantha. But she didn't take a step toward him. For a long moment she was transfixed by the breadth of his chest and his well-conditioned muscles. They conveyed a sense of strength and power, and yet she knew of Brock's gentleness when he held her so tenderly against his chest.

Her gaze moved up from his trim waist to his broad shoulders to his mouth, curved in a sexy smile. She was more worried about her keeping the distance.

"I'll turn around while you undress."

His smile captured her full attention; the meaning of his words didn't register.

He had to take the few steps between them and place his shirt in her hand. When he turned his back, Samantha finally moved, hurriedly stripping out of her dirty clothes and slipping into his oversized shirt. His smell tantalized her senses, making her strongly aware of how alone she and Brock were and threatening to wipe away all strength to resist this attraction she felt toward him.

"I'm through," she murmured when she had finished securing the last button on his shirt.

He slowly faced her, dressed only in his pants. She stood a foot from him, dressed only in his shirt, her clothes lying in a pile at her feet. As they stared at each other, Samantha's breath caught, and her blood rushed through her body like the wind through the trees.

He was everything she had always thought she didn't want in a man, and yet she was drawn to him as she had never been to any other man. She didn't understand these feelings deep inside her. She didn't understand herself anymore. Before she had always thought she had a good idea of what she wanted from life, how she felt, but now, everything was changing.

It would be so easy to take the one step toward him, Samantha realized. But emotionally she was torn in two. She wanted him, and yet she knew how dangerous that would be. She needed to cling to civilization because he was beginning to sway her toward the wild tamelessness of her surroundings.

She looked away, quickly picked up her clothes, and started for the river. She took her frustration out on her clothes, beating them against the rocks until she wasn't sure they would hold together when she put them back

164

on. She avoided looking at Brock because never in her life had her willpower been so lacking. She had always prided herself on her strong willpower, but as with so many things in the last week, she was discovering that was changing too.

Samantha decided to bathe as best she could at the water's edge, since all she had ever mastered was the dog paddle. She spread her clothes out to dry in the hot sun, then straightened.

Her gaze was immediately drawn to Brock, who was shaving without the benefit of a mirror. She watched him scrape the lather off one side of his face. He did it, as he did everything else, with an ease and naturalness that spoke of his self-confidence.

"I have a small compact mirror you can use," Samantha said.

"Will you hold it for me?"

"How did you manage when you traveled in the jungle before?" She held the mirror up before him, trying to ignore the quickening of her heartbeat.

"I always let my beard grow."

"Then why not now?"

He paused, his razor suspended in midair. "Because I saw your red skin after I kissed you."

He began to shave again, but shocked by his

165

answer, she dropped her hand to her side. He nicked himself with the straightedge.

"Oh, I'm sorry."

She touched his cheek to wipe away the spot of blood, but he seized her hand and held it flat against his face. She felt the smoothness of cleanly shaved skin and the warmth that radiated from him.

"We both know it won't be the last time we kiss, Sam."

She wanted to deny his words, but she couldn't. He only spoke the truth.

"I've seen you fighting what's between us. Give in to your feelings for once."

"Feelings! What's between us is pure lust." She yanked her hand from his grasp and thrust the mirror at him. "Manage by yourself."

As she stalked off toward the river, she heard his laughter. Fuming, she went farther into the water than she normally would. The river suddenly dropped off and she found herself submerged. She came up fighting, and instinctively started to dog-paddle the few feet to shallow water.

Embarrassed at his perception, angry at his male confidence, and confused by her conflicting emotions, Samantha started "washing" herself, aware of his wet shirt clinging to the outline of her body and leaving nothing to the imagination.

When she was through, she sat on a rock with

her compact mirror between her knees and began to apply her makeup, wincing when she spied the new crop of freckles on her nose. As she was putting on a light foundation, she wondered if she was losing her mind. Applying makeup in the middle of nowhere? And yet, it had become important, not because Brock was a yard away—he had seen her at her worst— but because it was one of the few links to her other life, to civilization thousands of miles away.

After she had completed that task, she undid the bun on top of her head and brushed her hair until it was completely dried. She was tempted to leave it down, remembering Brock's comment, but for practical reasons she put her hair back up in a bun. Obviously she wasn't totally losing her mind.

By the time they were ready to begin their journey down the river again, Samantha's clothes were dry, and she gladly gave Brock his shirt back, wishing she could distance herself emotionally and physically from him as easily as shedding his shirt. At least now she felt cleaner and more refreshed, though she knew it wouldn't last. For a short time she was the old Samantha Prince, bookstore owner from New Orleans.

Back on the river silence reigned between them, and Samantha went back to counting the different birds she saw as well as the different trees along the shore. The repetition was lulling her to sleep when she was jarred by a sharp movement. She opened her eyes to find the water churning and rushing around the raft. They had entered some rapids!

"What do I do?" she asked.

"Hang on."

She did, but she was vulnerably conscious of the fact that neither of them had a life preserver. Her gaze riveted on Brock as he fought to keep the raft from smashing into the rocks or turning over.

She could see the end of the rapids when the raft seemed to be lifted right out of the water. It came down on one side, tossing her out like unwanted baggage. Water engulfed her, pulling her down into the black depths of the river.

CHAPTER TEN

Rushing.

Tumbling.

Floating.

Then warmth enveloped Samantha. She was sinking into the sweet sensations of a dark void when rough hands pressed down on her chest. Fingers pried her lips apart and an insistent mouth breathed into hers.

"Live! Dammit, live!"

She was seized by a violent fit of coughing. Wrenched from the blissful darkness and peace that was beckoning her, she pushed at the rough hands, wanting to return to the black void.

"That's my girl. Fight."

She turned her face away from the insistent mouth as she coughed up river water. The rough hands took her into a gentle embrace, and she slowly eased her eyelids open against the glare of an intense sun. She felt as though a truck had mowed her down and somehow she had managed to survive the collision.

"Thank God you're alive, Samantha. Are you hurt?"

Suddenly everything came back to her. She had gone overboard while they had been riding the rapids. She had been drowning when . . .

"Sam?" Brock pulled back to look down at her.

She attempted a smile and thought she had never seen such a wonderful sight as Brock's face. "Let's put it this way. I know I'm alive. Every part of my body is telling me just how alive I am."

Brock laughed and hugged her to him, more tightly this time. "It's so good to hear you talking. For a minute there I didn't think I would. You certainly gave me a scare I don't wish to relive anytime soon."

"It'll be a while before I'll attempt that ride again, but I think I'm okay."

His hands ran down her arms, then the rest of her, caressing her as they moved over every inch of her body. "I don't think you broke anything."

"Just checking, sir?" She pushed away, filled with an intense desire to laugh for the sheer pleasure of having faced death and made it through relatively unscathed.

"Someone has to." His eyes sparkled as he smiled.

"And you elected yourself?"

"Guilty as charged." He tilted his head in a slight, mocking nod.

For the first time Samantha took a look around to see where they were. The rapids ended about a hundred feet upstream and they were sitting on an outcropping of rocks with trees on one side and the river on the other. The noise of the rapids in the background underscored in Samantha's mind the frequent stillness of the world they had entered.

"Where's the raft?"

Brock frowned.

"Mark's book! It's in my bag in the raft!" Panic replaced the languor she had begun to feel after that hair-raising ride.

"Calm down. The raft is tied up below the rock, but there's a hole in the side. It's losing air. We won't be able to use it anymore."

"We've got to get everything out. We've come too far to lose the book now." Samantha started to rise, but the green of the jungle and the color of the water blurred together to form one hue. She sank back down and closed her eyes to the spinning world.

"It'll be there in a few minutes, Sam. Take it easy. I'll get everything, you just rest."

While Brock climbed down to the river's edge to empty the ruined raft, Samantha brooded. Brock had come to her rescue, and she had found herself dependent on him yet again. While she realized she was in an alien environment and wasn't expected to be able to do everything correctly, she felt her self-confidence wavering. She had always been self-efficient, but now she was floundering as though there really was a new Samantha Prince emerging in the Amazon who had to relearn everything.

No. She was the same. The environment was the only thing different.

She wasn't going to allow herself to reflect on her near death. Until she had come to Brazil, she had never been required to be brave. She was discovering courage in herself, and that aspect of the new Samantha Prince—if she was indeed changing—pleased her.

When she returned to New Orleans, she was going to sign up for swimming lessons, she decided. She was never going to put herself in this type of situation again—not that there were that many rapids in the city of New Orleans, she thought with a laugh, mentally shaking off her melancholy.

"Everything is fine, Sam. Damp but still intact." Brock placed her canvas bag beside her, then sat down. "Feeling better?"

She nodded. "What are we going to do now?"

"Walk. This river eventually leads to the Rio

172

Negro, which will lead us to Manaus. I don't need to tell you it won't be easy, Samantha, but when we get to a main river, we can hitch a ride on a steamer heading for Manaus."

She was surprised by his using her full name yet a second time in less than fifteen minutes, and it took a few seconds for her to reply, "If it has to be done, I'll do it."

His eyes softened as his finger caressed her cheek. "I know. You're one tough lady. Out there in the river I thought I'd lost you, but you kept fighting your way to the top. Once we were finally past the rapids I was able to drag you into the raft."

"For a man who professes not to want to rescue damsels in distress, you've done more than your share."

"We're in this together whether you or I like it or not. I'm not some kind of hero, I just did what had to be done. That's all," he replied, a sharpness to his words.

Angered by his rebuke, she asked, "Do you have some kind of problem with being a hero? You're doing your damndest to declare you're not one while at the same time you're rescuing me from one dangerous situation after another."

"Heroes are for the books you love to read so much. In real life there are just plain, ordinary men and women."

Plain! Brock could never be described as

173

plain or ordinary. That would be like saying Renoir was just another man with a paintbrush. "So I should lump you in with Carlos and Paul? Just another man like them?" she asked sarcastically. Samantha pushed herself slowly to her feet, and this time she didn't feel dizzy.

"I'm not a hero, and I wish to hell you'd stop confusing me with one!" He shot to his feet and towered over her.

Her eyes glittered, her fingernails dug into the palms of her hands. "You don't have to worry about that, Mr. Slader. My brain isn't that waterlogged from my dunk in the river!"

She would love to storm away, but there was no place to go. She was forced to stand inches from him on a rock overlooking a rushing river, waiting for him to indicate where she should go. It was a frustrating experience for a woman who always controlled where she went and when she went there. In many ways she felt like a prisoner to the environment.

"I didn't want this job, lady, but I'll do what I have to to get you back safely to Manaus. Then we'll go our separate ways. Forget about the ten percent of that little black book. Ten percent of nothing is nothing."

She straightened, tilting her chin up in a defiant gesture. "Thank you. I'm so grateful for your kind help."

"Dammit! The last thing I want from you is

174

your gratitude," he replied in a voice that matched the temperature of his gaze.

"Then what do you want?" she asked him in an equally cold voice.

His piercing stare dissected her as though he were a botanist studying the local flora. He started to say something, then decided against it. Instead, a bland mask cloaked his expression, and he turned his back on her.

"I need to hack out a small clearing for us to set up camp. When I'm through, bring our things," he commanded in a hard tone.

Yes, master, she retorted silently. What did he want from her? Why wouldn't he answer her? Was he a superb actor, after all, and quick-thinking to come up with that story about being a geologist? Her head began to spin again with all her questions.

For the time being she had to accept what he had told her as the truth or she would drive herself crazy always suspecting everything he said or did. But she would hold one part of herself in reserve in case he was lying about who he was.

Brock was always the one telling her not to trust anyone. Maybe she should take his advice —but for different reasons. To love someone was to trust that person, but could she really trust him when she was so confused about who he was? Love? Damn, she didn't need any more complications. She quickly dismissed her train of thoughts.

Samantha sat back down on the rock and, with her legs drawn up close to her chest, waited for Brock to finish clearing a spot in the jungle. She wiped all thoughts and doubts from her mind and listened to his machete as it rhythmically struck the vines and branches behind her. The sound was hypnotic, and she dozed with her head on her knees, her arms entwined loosely about her legs.

By the time he was through, Samantha's clothes were dried by the tropical sun, and she felt refreshed by the short nap she had taken, almost prepared to confront him—almost.

She brought their things the short distance into the jungle, the shade of the tall trees a comfort after the glare of the harsh sun. Silently they went about their separate tasks. Brock hunted for their dinner while Samantha made the fire and slung the hammocks.

The tension between them was heavy with unspoken emotions, but Samantha was determined to keep her distance. She had to, because she didn't know what she felt anymore. Brock Slader had a way of overwhelming her and turning her rational thoughts into a jumbled mess.

They ate their dinner in the same stifling silence. Occasionally Samantha chanced a look at Brock, but he was staring at the fire. She sensed he was wrestling with some inner dilemma. That perhaps was the only thing they had in common, she decided, rising to her feet to go to bed. Unless she was sick, she never went to bed before eleven in New Orleans, but in the jungle a person geared his life to the movement of the sun.

Brock broke the silence. "Good night, Sam."

She paused by the fire and decided to ask one of the questions she had been thinking. "Now that we're on foot, how much longer will it be till we reach Manaus?"

"*Amanhã.*"

"*Amanhã?* What's that supposed to mean?"

"Here it means anywhere between tomorrow and next year." His expression gentled into a smile. "I don't know how long, Sam. Probably more than a week is all I can say."

She walked to her hammock and laid down, pulling the net over her. Three days ago she would have been extremely upset by what Brock had just told her. But now she accepted it with a surprising calm because there was nothing she could do about it. She was learning there was no planning in the jungle. She had to take things as they came. There was an order to this world, but it was nothing like what she was used to. The order centered around nature, not man.

She fell asleep, strangely composed, more

resigned to her situation than she would ever have thought possible.

A sound from hell filled the night. Samantha was torn from a deep sleep and flung into the world of darkness. She sat up and swung her legs over the hammock's edge. In the dim light of the fire she saw Brock still sitting there, and her fright was eased as it always was around him.

Continuous roars blended into one long tormenting sound, sending a terrifying chill up Samantha's spine. She quickly moved to the fire, feeling a lot safer by its protective flames and in Brock's presence.

"What's that?" she asked in a shaky voice.

"Howler monkeys."

"Monkeys? It sounds like a chorus of demons shouting at each other."

"There are two clans battling vocally."

"The sound should be taped for a horror movie. How long will this go on?"

"Until one backs off. Possibly hours."

"At least I've never been one to require a lot of sleep." Samantha sat down across from Brock and looked over the flames toward him.

"Neither have I."

"Ah, we've found common ground," she said lightly, wanting to erase the tension that had developed earlier. They had a long way to go, and being a practical person, Samantha realized it would be easier if they were on friendly terms.

"If we searched long enough, I knew we would," he replied, smiling for the first time in hours.

"I have a favor to ask."

Brock arched a brow.

"Okay, another favor," Samantha amended. "While we're strolling through the jungle, will you teach me about it? I want to learn. That's part of the reason I love to read so much. I love to learn about different things. In fact, there isn't anything I can think of that I wouldn't be interested in."

"Snakes?"

Samantha laughed. "Well, possibly snakes, but even they are fascinating creatures. Maybe if I learned about them, I could appreciate them. I suppose anything is possible. This will be a perfect opportunity to experience something firsthand, as you've suggested."

For a few seconds surprise flickered into his eyes, but he quickly concealed it and replied, "I would love to show you the delights of my life-style."

She hadn't fully realized until she had asked him to teach her about the Amazon that she had accepted her situation and was going to make the best of it. Now, in several ways, she looked forward to the next week, because with her acceptance came a peace and relaxation she hadn't experienced before.

"I want to learn how to survive in the jungle. I want to learn which foods to eat and which ones to avoid. You talked about swarming a tree. Will you teach me how?"

"It's not easy."

"I know. But it's one way you gather food. So much is up in the trees, out of reach. There are a lot of animals that a person can't even see from below, living hundreds of feet off the ground."

"Okay. If you're sure?"

She nodded.

Suddenly the jungle was quiet, the only sounds those of the crackling fire and the different insects that Samantha had learned from the beginning to tune out.

"I guess we'd better get as much sleep as possible," Samantha murmured, her gaze trapped by Brock's.

"Yes, I guess so."

Neither moved.

"Brock, I don't think of you as a hero. In fact, you're very different from my imagined hero."

He stared at her for another full minute, then chuckled. "I'm not sure if that's a compliment or a complaint."

"Neither. Just a fact." She paused, swallowed several times, and continued, "I am grateful to you for saving my life on more than one occasion, but I feel more than gratitude."

"What are your feelings?"

"As confusing as I suspect yours are. Am I right?"

"When I returned to Manaus from my previous expedition into the jungle, the last thing in the world I wanted was anything—or anyone—to complicate my life. I can't say my life has been simple the past few days."

"You still have ten percent of whatever is in the black book. I believe my brother when he said it was valuable, Brock. You'll have your money for your oil deal. That's the least I can do for you."

"Gratitude again?"

"No, I'm just keeping my promise to you when we began this journey."

"A business arrangement, pure and simple?"

"Don't you think that's the wisest?"

"Believe it or not, I do. I want to keep everything as simple as possible under the circumstances. My life is now based on no ties, on complete freedom to move when and where I want to."

"While my life is in New Orleans running a bookstore from ten in the morning to six in the evening."

"Orderly, neat, precise." He was reminding her of their basic differences.

"Right." She rose. "I'm glad we agree. No

complications in our personal lives. Strictly business between us."

"Agreed."

"Good night for the second and I hope the last time tonight."

He didn't reply and he didn't go to his hammock. He was still sitting by the fire when Samantha fell asleep again.

True to his word, Samantha learned from Brock as they trekked through the Amazon over the next several days. An appreciation for the primal beauty of her surroundings grew as the days passed. They journeyed through thick jungle with trees over a hundred feet tall shielding them from the sun's intense rays.

Lianas, like boa constrictors, entwined themselves around trunks while the trees' roots snaked along the surprisingly clean ground. There were no dank or oppressive odors, because Samantha found very little rotting. The jungle, its greenery sprinkled with a vivid array of colors, filled her with wonder.

Ferns, vines, air plants, dripped from the trees as well as moisture. Samantha was bathed in sweat in less than an hour after they started in the morning. Everything about her seemed to be always wet from the rain, and she learned to accept that as well as many other things; their slow pace, the horde of insects, the dim light even though it was daytime.

182

Samantha discovered Brock's patience as he stopped innumerable times to point out a sapphire hummingbird, a column of soldier ants, or a plant used as a contraceptive by the Indian women. She stretched it to the limit with her questions and attempts at learning how to do something.

The first evening they set up camp, he took her hunting and taught her to swarm a tree. She inched her way up ten feet and fell, but Brock eased her fall. They rolled on the ground and started laughing. She repeated her attempt until she was exhausted, but she had climbed fifteen feet and was determined to double that in the next few days and reach the fruit.

During the fourth day they briefly left the thick foliage and emerged on a savannah. Samantha immediately put on her straw hat, which wouldn't have won any awards for fashion, having survived the river and the cramped quarters of her canvas bag. The sunlight hurt her eyes, and it took several moments before she could see well enough to walk.

While traversing the savannah, Samantha saw a jet fly overhead and wondered about the people on the plane. Where were they going? What would they have for dinner? Were they listening to music or watching a movie? Were they curled up in a blanket because the air-conditioned cabin was too cold?

For the first time in four days she longed for the simple luxuries of civilization that she had always taken for granted. Then they were engulfed by the semidarkness of the rain forest again, and she forgot about the jet overhead and listened to Brock explain yet another unusual plant.

The evening of the fourth night they stopped at a place already cleared and slung their hammocks. After they gathered wood for the fire, she and Brock went hunting. For the first time Samantha made it to the top of a tree and cut the fruit.

Proud of her accomplishment, she returned to the forest floor to find Brock leaning heavily against a tree trunk. His face was unusually pale beneath his tanned skin, and sweat trickled down his face.

"Are you all right?" Samantha asked, picking up the pieces of fruit she had dropped from the treetop.

"Fine. Let's head back. This is enough for tonight." He wiped his forehead and shoved away from the tree trunk.

Back in camp, Brock didn't say a word, and Samantha's concern intensified. They roasted the Brazil nuts and finished off the dried meat from Brock's hunt the first night in the forest. She tried to draw him out, but after dinner he announced he was going to sleep early.

Samantha sat by the fire and watched Brock

slowly walk to his hammock and lie down. Maybe he was just tired. After all, he went to sleep after she did every night and was up before she was in the morning. She prayed that was the only thing wrong.

After putting more wood on the fire, Samantha turned in too. But around midnight her sleep was disturbed. Opening her eyes, she listened.

A moan drifted through the night.

She sat up in her hammock and looked toward Brock's. Another moan penetrated the stillness. Brock pushed his netting off as though he were fighting off an attacker.

Samantha hurried over to replace the netting which protected them from the numerous insects. His body was drenched in sweat, his forehead was hot. He moaned again and shoved her hand away.

Paralyzed, Samantha stared down at Brock thrashing about in his hammock, a fever raging through his body. She had never felt so helpless in her life.

CHAPTER ELEVEN

As Samantha tried to decide what she could do to help him, Brock's eyes opened and he stared back at her. A feverish pain was reflected in them and it tore at her.

Focusing on her, he ran his tongue over parched lips and whispered, "Malaria. Medicine in backpack."

With trembling hands Samantha rummaged through his backpack until she found the bottle of medicine. She had heard malaria was a common disease in the tropics, but she really knew very little about it except that it was transmitted by mosquito, of which the Amazon had more than its share.

She gave him the bottle and some water left over from dinner. With her assistance he sat up, his hands shaking worse than hers.

"How many tablets?" she asked as she cradled him against her and opened the bottle.

"Two."

She emptied two tablets from the bottle and

put one after another into his mouth between sips of water. After he'd eased back down, Samantha felt his forehead again. It was even hotter than before. She feared his malaria was progressing rapidly, and again she experienced that overwhelming helplessness.

Using some of the remaining water, she bathed his face but almost immediately he was covered in sweat again. Not knowing if it even helped to cleanse him, she unbuttoned his shirt and washed his chest and neck, feeling his trembling body beneath her hand.

He seemed to be slipping into another world, controlled by the fever, never comfortable in any position for more than a few seconds. As though they were hot pokers, he lashed out at her hands that were touching him.

"Emma! Don't!" The words, more like a groan, were wrenched from him.

Samantha, shocked by the unfamiliar name, started to straighten away from him, but Brock gripped her hand and held her close.

"We can work it out."

Work what out? Who was Emma? Samantha wondered as Brock's fingers bit into her wrist.

Pain glazed his eyes as he stared up at her, not really seeing. Her hand felt numb from his grasp, but she could do nothing to break the manacle about her. Every time she tried to pull

187

away, his fingers tightened even more, until she feared he would break her wrist.

Then suddenly his eyelids closed, his body went slack, and his hand fell to his side. Samantha took a step away, rubbing her wrist to get the blood flowing into her numb hand.

His hallucination, produced by the high fever, opened a whole new avenue of questions for Samantha. Every time she began to think she knew Brock Slader, something else would happen to show her just how little she really did know. That realization was disconcerting, renewing all her previous doubts.

Brock appeared calmer, and Samantha approached his hammock to feel his forehead. He was still very hot and soaking with perspiration. She again bathed his skin, trying to cool him. He didn't object this time.

When she felt she had done all she could for him, she moved to the fire to add more wood and sit, waiting to see if the medicine helped. Every few minutes she was up to check on Brock and wipe his face and lips with a cool piece of cloth.

Was this a recurring malaria attack or had he contracted it since they had been in the jungle? She knew so little about Brock that she didn't even know how long he had been in the Amazon or if he had these feverish episodes often.

Her sense of total isolation grew as the minutes passed into hour by slow hour. The eerie darkness about their camp seemed to close in on Samantha, black walls that became menacing as she scanned them for signs of night predators. She added even more wood to the fire until it blazed high. The fire made her feel a little better.

Between her intervals of bathing Brock, she went to his pile of belongings and picked up his machete for protection. The sense that she needed protection arose more from her vivid imagination than from anything the jungle had to offer, but she did feel more secure with it in her hand.

By the time dawn of the second day fingered its way through the forest canopy, illuminating the rain forest in a dim light, Brock had finally quieted into a deep sleep. Samantha stood over his hammock, watching him and feeling as if she had gone through the sweating and thrashing with him. Her body ached with exhaustion and fear.

Slipping her hand under the netting, she caressed his face, smoothing a lock of damp hair from his forehead. His skin had cooled in the last hour, but it was still warm with fever.

She glanced at her hammock and thought briefly that she should get some sleep, but there was so much she had to do. She had no idea how long they would be there, and they would need food as well as more firewood and water. This was the first time she felt that she could leave the camp long enough to get those necessities.

As she gathered Brock's machete and knife, she was thankful that she had insisted on learning something about the jungle. It gave her the confidence she needed to go alone into the thick rain forest to look for food. It was up to her to get them through the next day or so, and that thought both excited and frightened her.

Samantha collected nuts from the buriti palm tree and some vines with water in them. She decided she would make a cold protein-rich soup from nuts, as Brock had taught her the second day in the jungle. He would need as much liquid as she could get him to drink. She feared he would dehydrate if he kept sweating the way he was, and she could store the liquid in the hollowed-out fruit shells that Brock had made into bowls.

When she returned to camp, Brock was still asleep. After feeling his face to make sure his fever wasn't out of control again, she prepared the soup and had some while she waited to see if Brock would awaken. When he didn't, she decided to get some rest before collecting the firewood.

She had spent the last thirty-six hours pacing their small clearing, her nerves taut, her emotions on hold as she waited out the fever. If she didn't take care of herself, she would end up as weak as Brock. The jungle was harsh on a person's body, and she had better remember that.

She fell asleep almost instantly and didn't awaken until she felt her hammock swing. When she opened her eyes, she discovered Brock, looking like hell, standing over her, his hand gripping the edge of the hammock. She took in his dull eyes, his unruly hair, his sweat-drenched clothes, and decided she had never beheld a more wonderful sight. He was standing over her on his own two feet, a bit shaky, but at least upright.

"What are you doing out of bed?" she finally asked as she hurriedly climbed from her hammock, slipping her arm about him to help support his weight.

"When you didn't answer me, I began to worry." He swayed into her and clutched her arm to keep his balance.

Samantha staggered back under his weight, but she managed to steady both of them. "It's not me you need to worry about. Let's get you back to bed."

"I'm fine now. I just had to sweat the fever out."

"Oh, so you think it's time to push on?"

"We have to."

"Brock Slader, I'm not about to start out and have you collapse on me when we don't have the luxuries of this camp. I won't leave before tomorrow—if then. Now, let's get you back to

191

bed and no more talk about leaving. I don't take kindly to mutiny."

A chuckle rumbled in his chest, but Brock leaned heavily on her and allowed her to escort him back to his hammock. "You would have been a perfect drill sergeant. If you ever want to give up your bookstore, I'm sure the army could use you."

"Give up my bookstore? Never! I saved for years so I could buy it. I'm my own boss and I deal in something I love, books. I call that a perfect job."

"A perfect life."

Samantha looked sharply at Brock, for beneath his words she heard a sarcastic edge. "I don't have any complaints about my life in New Orleans."

"How about your life in the Amazon?" Brock eased back onto the hammock, a silver gleam lightening his dull eyes.

"This"—her arm swept wide to indicate the campsite—"might appear in *Better Homes and Gardens* on the ten worst list if they had one."

"Oh, I don't know. Our garden is one of nature's finest. Probably something like the Garden of Eden, wild and lush, with anything a man could want."

She felt his intense gaze on her. "I made some soup. I'll get you some."

Samantha purposely avoided eye contact with him because she knew that teasing tone in

192

his voice. He was definitely on the road to recovery, she decided as she poured him some soup. She suspected nothing got him down for long—not even malaria.

She returned to his hammock and helped him sit up, even though he gave her a look that said he could do it himself. "Have you had malaria before?" she asked.

"Yes. Every once and a while I'm fortunate enough to have a recurring bout. I always carry my medicine, so it usually isn't too bad."

"Isn't too bad? You scared me to death. I wasn't sure if you'd make it. I've never seen a fever like that."

"Nothing like the first time. I almost died."

Her heart skipped a beat, then began to pound against her breast. She wouldn't let herself think about the possibility of Brock's dying. She hadn't while he was feverish and she wouldn't now. She turned away and busied herself with gathering some wood. When she was through and had restarted a fire, she finally approached him.

"Did you need anything else?" Her eyes locked with his.

"Some water."

"Oh, I'm sorry. You're probably dying of thirst."

"Actually, I want to shave."

Samantha blushed, remembering when he

193

had told her why he was shaving. "I'll get some at the river."

"No. Just help me to the river. I'll shave there and wash up."

She stared at him suspiciously. Help him to the river? His helplessness was sudden, and he was definitely up to something.

"Sam, it will be getting dark soon. We'd better hurry."

When he stood, she placed her arm about his waist and he put his arm about hers. The distance to the river was no more than a hundred feet, but the whole way there Brock's body was plastered against hers, making her alarmingly aware of his male presence.

At the river he removed his damp shirt and had started to take off his pants when Samantha exclaimed, "What are you doing?"

"Going for a swim."

"You're too weak. I can't swim."

He grinned. "What's that got to do with it?"

"If you fainted or something, I couldn't save you."

"I've never fainted in my life. If it will make you feel better, I'll only go a few feet from shore where I can stand up. But I feel grimy and this water looks great. Care to join me?"

"No," she answered quickly, wanting to look away from Brock as he stripped down to his underwear and yet not about to look away.

She told herself the reason she was staying to

watch was in case he did become lightheaded, but she wasn't really kidding herself. She was transfixed by the muscled prowess of his body as he moved toward the water. His well-proportioned build held a masculine grace that was hypnotic to watch.

"It really is nice, Sam," Brock called out before he dipped his whole body into the water.

Samantha had to acknowledge that it looked heavenly and she felt as grimy as he did. Even with the daily rain showers, the perspiration always made her feel she wasn't quite clean. If she stripped down to her underwear, she would still be decent. In fact, many bathing suits revealed more than her underwear would. She looked around as though she expected someone to be hiding in the bushes.

Then, before she had time to debate the wisdom of joining Brock in the river with only her underwear on, she discarded her pants and shirt and stepped into the water up to her knees. She had to agree with Brock. The water was cool and refreshing, washing away the perspiration and dirt.

When something brushed against her leg, she jumped back, whirling around at the same time to see what it was. Brock, with water dripping off his beautifully built body, straightened out of the water with a big grin on his face. Samantha had a strong urge to strangle him.

"I think you enjoy scaring me to death. I thought you were a school of piranhas."

"Relax, Sam. You're standing straighter than a soldier does at attention. The river is pretty shallow here. You can come out farther."

"No!" She stood her ground, resisting the hand that Brock offered.

"Which are you more frightened of, the water or me?"

"Don't flatter yourself," she retorted, and wondered about the answer to that question herself.

"I think it's time you learned to swim, Sam. I'll teach you."

"No!" She started back toward shore, deciding that she was clean enough and much too vulnerable, dressed so scantily.

"Why not? You don't strike me as a woman who runs from something."

She spun about in a few inches of water, her hands resting on her waist. "Drop it, Slader."

He moved slowly toward Samantha, as though he were stalking her. "Why not? I can be as curious as you. What happened to make you afraid of water?"

For a few seconds she was whisked back to another time when she was six and at the beach with her parents. She didn't even see Brock cover the remaining feet between them. Suddenly he was in front of her and his masculine

196

scent chased away all other smells and dominated her senses.

"What happened?" he probed gently.

"My father drowned at the beach when I was six. Dad was trying to save someone else, a stranger, and he got caught in the undertow."

Brock's arms went about her and their wet bodies meshed. "Don't you see that's the best reason in the world to learn to swim, Samantha?"

She nodded against his chest. "I've tried. I freeze up in the water. I keep seeing my father going under."

"You can do a pretty mean dog paddle."

"That was my survival instinct at work. I avoid water if possible."

"Come on. It's hard to avoid water in the jungle, especially during the rainy season." Brock cradled her against him and led her farther into the river. "I want you to float on your back. I'll hold you up. But the main thing I want you to do is relax completely."

"Relax?"

"Trust me, Samantha. I won't let anything happen to you."

Trust me, Samantha. Those words echoed through her mind as she lay stiffly in the water with Brock's arms supporting her. Could she trust him? Her heart said yes; her mind wasn't sure.

"Relax or it won't work."

Samantha stared up at Brock, who was smiling tenderly down at her. She willed her body to relax, and by concentrating on Brock and his concern, muscle by muscle she did.

"Close your eyes."

Samantha did as Brock commanded.

"Think of nothing but nice things. Think of home. Think of a thick, juicy steak and a baked potato dripping piled with butter and sour cream."

Samantha thought of Brock, with his arms about her, kissing her until she forgot about home, about everything in life but him. In her daydreaming she felt as if she were floating on a cloud without a care in the world.

She opened her eyes, expecting to find Brock hovering over her, but he was standing a few feet away and she was floating on her back alone. Immediately her body tensed and she started to sink. She stood quickly before taking in a mouth full of river water.

"For two minutes you were on your own, Sam. You can do it."

"For a person who for thirty-six hours didn't seem likely to make it, you certainly are fit now."

"I can't afford to let a little thing like malaria get me down for long. Remember, we have people after us."

"I haven't forgotten." She waded past him

198

and out of the water to dry in the late-afternoon sun.

Lying down on the beach next to her, Brock said, "I think we only have a few days until we reach a village where we can pick up a steamer heading for Manaus."

Trying to ignore the fact that they were both dressed in very little, Samantha said, "Good. I know Mark is alive from what Carlos and Paul said that night at the mission. When we find my brother, he can tell us what's in the book and you can have your share of whatever it is."

"It won't be that simple, Sam. First we have to find your brother. I'm not sure he wants to be found."

"Nonsense. I'm his sister. Why would he hide from me?" she asked, not having succeeded in ignoring their attire. It was impossible with Brock so close that she could touch him with no effort at all.

"You might be watched in Manaus for the very reason you could lead the people after us to your brother."

"Then we'll have to make sure we're not watched. We don't have to stay at the Grand Hotel."

"We?"

Samantha turned to look at Brock. "I assumed you wanted to be in this to the end for your share."

"Don't ever assume anything, Sam." A bitter

edge entered his voice; a hard glint flashed in his eyes.

For a moment she was hurt by his words. She had assumed a lot where Brock was concerned, she realized. He was right; she couldn't assume anything. *"I'll* think of some way to get in touch with Mark without anyone finding out. He's the key."

"We will think of a way. In this case you were right to assume that I'll be in it till the end. After all, I've invested a lot of time not to be paid."

"Right." Samantha jumped to her feet and gathered up her clothes to dress. She was trying desperately to keep the pain at bay, but it was growing rapidly. Why was it so important that Brock just want to help her for herself? Because she was falling in love with him in spite of all her logical reasons not to, and he was everything she didn't want in a man. The realization struck her like a stunning blow, and she nearly dropped her pile of clothes.

Brock was on his feet and in front of her, blocking her escape. "You said so yourself, Sam. It's better if it's strictly business between us. Are you having second thoughts now?"

She kept her expression neutral as she stared up at him. "No." She pushed past him, dressing as she made her way toward their camp.

She was kidding herself. Things had gone

beyond business and she didn't see any way out of this mess without being hurt terribly.

Back at camp she waited for Brock to appear behind her, but when he didn't come, she feared he had fainted or something and quickly retraced her steps to the river. He stood at the edge of the water, dressed, with his hands stuffed into his back pockets. He was staring down at the river flowing past him.

Samantha had started to leave when Brock said, "This is the time of day I like best."

She made her way to his side, acknowledging the beauty of the sunset. The river was tinted a purplish red, reflecting the setting sun in its swiftly moving waters. A towering tree, standing proudly alone above the rest, was dark against a deep purple sky laced with streaks of golden and orange lights. The tree reminded Samantha of Brock, proud, erect, a loner, needing no one.

He slipped his arm about her shoulders. "We both know we've gone beyond being just business partners."

She nodded, fighting tears and the lump in her throat.

"When two people are thrown together, as you and I have been, everything is heightened. When you return to New Orleans and your normal life, though, you'll eventually forget the adventure we had. It will become like one of those books you've read. Before long you won't even remember characters' names or locales."

In one respect he was right about their adventure's becoming like a book she'd read. She would treasure it, savoring the important parts over and over on lonely nights. The main character would never fade from her thoughts, she strongly suspected, because he had left a mark on her that was rare for a book but occasionally possible. Who could forget characters like Rhett Butler or Romeo?

"Who is Emma? Your sister?" The question had been in the back of Samantha's mind ever since he had said the name in his feverish state.

His arm on her shoulders tensed. He inhaled sharply. "Where did you hear that name?"

"From you. While you had your fever."

For long moments he didn't say anything but continued to stare at the river. The sky darkened, the shadows of night enclosing them.

"Emma is my ex-wife."

She wanted him to continue; she wanted him to tell her he didn't care about Emma anymore. She waited.

A shriek sounded in the night. Samantha tensed.

"It's only a macaw. But we should get back to camp where it's safer."

Brock walked ahead of Samantha, but they

were linked together by their clasped hands. Samantha had hoped he would tell her more about himself, but in camp he immediately started building up the fire and preparing something to eat, as though he were looking for something to keep himself busy.

Seated by the fire while they ate, Samantha avoided looking at him. He was trying to keep their relationship on a less personal level which in the long run was better for both of them, and she kept trying to get closer, to probe deeper into the man Brock Slader was. But even knowing in the end that the closer she was to Brock the more hurt she would endure when she left Brazil didn't make any difference. She wanted to know him on all levels.

Is Emma important to you? Are you still in love with your ex-wife? "How long have you been divorced?" was the question that Samantha finally asked.

"Seven years." Brock rose, his look shuttered. "Now, if you'll excuse me, Sam, I need some rest if we're going to leave tomorrow morning."

"Yes, of course," she murmured, watching him walk to his hammock.

As before, she felt shut out of his life, and, Lord help her, she was in love with him. If he knew, she suspected he wouldn't even stay around to find out what the treasure was.

* * *

"This is a village? There are only four houses in it!" Samantha wasn't even sure she should call them houses—they were more like huts.

"This is a village because it's the only one for a fifty-mile radius. The important thing is that a steamer does stop here."

They entered the village cautiously at high noon. Brock had insisted they wait until everyone was taking a nap before showing themselves. He wanted to scout it out before approaching a villager.

"You stay here." He rubbed his half-grown beard, which he had let go for the last several days. "I look like someone who belongs in the jungle. You don't. I want to find out when the steamer will arrive."

Samantha hid in a grove of banana trees behind one of the houses. She expected Brock to be gone for a while, but he was back in a few minutes.

He pushed her further behind a tree, whispering, "Stay down. I think one of Carlos's men is in the village."

CHAPTER TWELVE

Terrific, Samantha thought despondently. Had they spent over a week trekking through the jungle only to have things end in a collection of four huts in the middle of nowhere?

The searing sun beat down on her and the air was still. Swatting at an insect, Samantha waited quietly while Brock decided on a course of action.

"We have to get to the river without being seen by him," Brock finally whispered, his body hugging close to Samantha's.

"Where is he?"

"Sitting in front of the house closest to the river. He has a hat pulled low over his head as if he's asleep, but I saw him lift his head and peer out, scanning the village."

"What if the whole village is helping him?"

"That's what I'm afraid of."

"How far is the next village?"

"Too far. And there could be someone waiting there too."

Alarmed by the idea that everywhere they went one of Carlos's men could be waiting, Samantha asked, "How big is Carlos's operation?"

"I don't know. That's why I'm worried. That man might be perfectly innocent. There's no sure way to tell, so we can't take any chances."

"What if we flag the riverboat down below the village and get on then? We'd be safe if no one who works for Carlos is riding the boat."

Brock thought a moment, staring at the four houses as if he could see into the huts to what was going on inside. "You may have a point. We have to take a chance on the steamer or it will be weeks before we can reach Manaus. And we're ill equipped to travel in the jungle for that length of time. Let's hope Carlos can't cover every base or that I'm being paranoid and no one is waiting for us."

"Do you know a place on the river where someone on the steamer might see us and pick us up?"

His eyes sparkled as they slowly took in her face. "Yes, I do. It's only a few hours from here." He gently touched her cheek with his forefinger. "We'll have to leave now and walk in the hottest part of the day. I don't know when the steamer will be arriving here. We could wait days, or we could miss it while we're walking."

"And we could get caught." She didn't want

to spend any more time than necessary in the jungle for the obvious reason that it wasn't a easy place on a novice like herself. But it also forced an intimacy between herself and Brock that made her dream, emotionally dangerous dreams that were going to leave her very hurt in the end.

"That's definitely a possibility." His fingertip whispered over her face.

"We have to do it. We have no other choice." Her skin tingled where Brock's finger skimmed over her, and she forgot all about the intense heat, the insects, and the man in the village.

"You're quite a lady, Samantha Prince."

The world seemed to stop for a few moments as Samantha gazed into Brock's eyes that gently caressed her from their smoky depths. Her attention became absorbed in every minute detail of his features. The fullness of his lips, the roughness of his beard, the warmth of his silver-gray eyes, were all she cared about.

She wanted to tell him he was quite a man, but the moment passed and the sensual gleam in his eyes faded. His usual shuttered look descended as he straightened away from her.

"We have no time to waste."

They followed the river for three hours before Brock stopped and pointed out toward the water. "The riverboat will have to come in close to shore here. Hopefully someone on board will see us signaling."

"How will we get to the boat?"

"Swim."

"I was afraid you were going to say that." Samantha shielded her eyes with her hand and scanned the river. She'd only had one swimming lesson and certainly wasn't ready for the big test yet. "Maybe we should have taken our chances at the village."

"You'll do fine, Sam."

"Because I have no other choice," she finished, laughter in her voice. She was doing a lot of things she hadn't thought herself capable of two weeks before because there was no other choice, but it helped to know that Brock had faith in her.

They positioned themselves on the bank to begin their watch. Samantha drew her knees up to her chest and clasped her arms around her legs. The breeze stirred wisps of her hair and cooled her sweat-covered skin as the sun descended toward the horizon. In between short, intense rainstorms the insects continued to love the taste of her skin and were holding a party on her.

"Do you miss your family living here?" She slapped a small insect that had come in for a landing.

"I keep in touch. I haven't been in the Amazon that long." He stretched his legs out and crossed them at his ankles, then leaned back and propped himself up on his elbows.

"How long?"

"Thirteen months."

"Where were you before Brazil?"

"Alaska."

"One frontier after another."

"You could say that." He pulled his hat low to conceal the expression in his eyes.

"Tell me about Emma. Did you start your world traveling after or before your divorce?" Though she couldn't see his face well, the slight tensing of his body told Samantha she was treading into dangerous territory. But having spent over a week in the jungle, she was a lot braver.

"After."

"Is she the reason?"

He pushed up the brim of his hat and sent her a sharp look that would have left most people speechless. But in the past week they had been through a lot—more than many people went through in a lifetime together.

"Are you running away from something or someone?" she persisted, determined to get inside of this man she knew little about.

"Why do people assume just because I reject their way of life that I'm running away?"

"You avoid the subject of Emma. You avoid the subject of yourself. Why?"

"The subject matter isn't suitable for an autobiography. A reader wouldn't get past the second page."

"This reader would."

Sitting up, he stared at the river again, lacing his fingers together until his knuckles whitened. "I suppose if I don't tell you the gory details I won't have a moment's peace." There was more resignation than anger in his voice.

"A mystery has always intrigued me."

"And if I take the mystery out of my life?"

She would still be intrigued, Samantha suddenly realized. But she remained quiet, not daring to reveal that bit of information.

He sighed. "I assumed Emma would understand my need to do something else with my life other than work for a large oil company and making a lot of money. I assumed wrong. Emma was accustomed to a certain life-style and she wanted it to remain that way. I've learned you can't change people just because you want it."

"You changed."

"In order to survive. Emma is a closed chapter."

"Not to be reread?"

"A waste of a person's time."

"A good book is meant to be savored many times."

"I wouldn't argue that with you. But with us the story was over before the final page. I was just too busy to see it." Brock paused, then said, "Tell me about this brother of yours."

"You are so good at changing the subject when it gets too hot."

"What does your brother do when he isn't getting himself into trouble?"

Laughing, she shook her head. She wasn't going to get anything else out of him, and she strongly suspected that, if he hadn't wanted her to know it in the first place, she would never have learned what she had.

"Whatever there is to do that interests my little brother," she finally answered. "Much like you. In fact, you two would probably get along well. Kindred souls."

"Has he been in Brazil long?"

"Two years. He lives in Rio. I'm not sure why he's in the Amazon."

"To find the lost city of gold?"

"Anything is possible with Mark. A challenge is everything to him. He attacks life with zeal, making sure nothing ties him down."

"Never worrying about the future? IRAs? Retirement?"

Her back stiffened and she glared at him. "Those are genuine concerns for many people."

"I've learned plans have a way of changing no matter how carefully you construct them. I had everything planned, my career, my mar-

211

riage. The only thing that I didn't figure in was that I would change."

"I may like things organized, but I'm not inflexible."

Brock chuckled. "No, you're not, at least not after this past week."

"Shock therapy can do wonders for a person," Samantha replied with a laugh.

Suddenly Brock was on his feet and waving his arms. Samantha looked toward the river to see a riverboat coming toward them, and she jumped up and began waving her arms too. They shouted as they ran down the bank toward the water.

"They don't look like they're stopping to pick up passengers," Samantha said, inhaling deeply to slow her labored breathing.

"They won't stop, only slow down. We'll have to swim out to them." Already in the water, Brock paused and turned back to her. "We only have a few minutes to make the connection or they'll go on by."

Samantha's eyes were round as she stared at the water between her and the steamer. When the boat passed the place where they were, it wouldn't be more than a hundred feet away from the shore, but to a nonswimmer it seemed like a mile.

"Sam! Come on!" Brock held out his hand for her.

Her legs felt rooted to the ground. She

212

wanted to pick them up; she couldn't. Brock hurried back and grabbed her hand, pulling her toward the river.

"Sam, you've got to swim. I'll be right next to you. Nothing is going to happen. We haven't come this far to have it all end."

Samantha listened to his soothing words as the water got deeper. Finally she could no longer walk but had to swim. And as before, she did what she had to do; all she thought about was the next stroke; all she focused on was the side of the steamer getting closer.

At the boat Samantha was the first one to grasp the rope flung over for them; then Brock did. Two men on board hauled her up with Brock right behind her. Safe, she sank to the deck, drawing in deep gulps of air. Her heart finally slowed its frantic beating.

The shore where they had sat quickly disappeared from her view as the steamer went around a bend. Their short swim couldn't have lasted more than a few minutes, but to Samantha it had seemed like a lifetime. Yet she had done it, and a sense of pride in her accomplishment filled her.

"I'm going to see the captain," Brock informed her, depositing their wet belongings next to her on the deck.

While Brock was gone, Samantha took a moment to look at the riverboat. It needed a coat of paint, but it appeared to be in good condi-

213

tion. There were two decks to the steamer, with cargo stowed on the lower one out in the open. A family of Brazilians was staring at her as though she were one of the legendary mermaids of the Amazon.

Did they work for Carlos? Did the two men that brought her on board work for Carlos? Samantha wondered. She hated the need to be suspicious of everyone she encountered. It wasn't in her nature, but that, too, she found she had to change in order to survive.

When Brock had been gone for an unusual amount of time, Samantha began to worry. What if someone was holding him captive? Or what if someone had deposed of him and she were all alone now with the black book?

The book! She had forgotten all about it. Quickly she rummaged through her canvas tote until she found her makeup bag. She checked it to see if the book was soaking wet like everything else. Thankfully the bag really was waterproof and the book was dry.

The sound of footsteps brought her head up, and she hurriedly stashed the book back in its hiding place. Brock and a stranger were approaching. She stood and hoped the stranger was the captain, not one of Carlos's men.

"We're in luck. The captain has a cabin for us." Brock slipped his arm about her, pulling her close. Whispering into her ear while it appeared as if he were kissing her, he added, "I told him we wanted privacy."

First the headhunters, now the captain, and soon the whole crew would think she was Brock's woman—everyone but Brock, she realized, wishing he thought it too. Shocked by the direction her thoughts were going, she decided she must have a walking case of malaria. Surely her thoughts were the result of a high fever.

The cabin was actually a room that barely fit two people and a bunk made for one. But at least it was a roof over her head and the bed wouldn't swing. The bunk even had a mattress that looked comfortable.

When the captain left, grinning from ear to ear, Brock said, "It isn't the *Queen Mary*, but it's home for the next few days."

"Well, I suppose we can spend most of our time out on deck," she said as she inspected the cramped quarters again.

"No, we can't."

"Why not? We can barely turn around in here without bumping into each other."

"I told the captain your father was looking for us, that we're running away to be married in Manaus."

"And he bought that!"

"That and a large amount of money to keep quiet. The less we're seen the better, Sam.

215

Most people along the river mind their own business, but it helps to give them a reason to."

"Out of sight, out of mind."

"Right."

After the wide open spaces of nature, Samantha feared she would get a good case of claustrophobia. What would they do with their time? Twiddle their thumbs?

"First, we should hang up any extra clothing that's in our bags so it can dry."

"Where?"

"I have some string we can use."

That task occupied their time for ten minutes, which left over forty-eight hours to go. With the clothes on her body only slightly damp now, Samantha sat on the bunk, leaning back against the wall, and watched Brock check his gun.

"Is it ruined?"

"Hopefully not." He replaced it in his backpack.

"But no one else will know if it's ruined, so if you need to use it, you can."

"If you point a gun at a person, you'd better be prepared to use it."

"Have you ever had to?"

"No, but then I've never had to run for my life."

"You said you like a challenge."

"Did I? Well, I think I've had my quota for the next five years."

Suddenly the boat stopped. Samantha tensed. "Why are we stopping?"

Brock looked out the porthole above her head. "I don't know. We're in the middle of the river." He moved closer to the window and opened it to get a better view. "There's a boat approaching us."

"Carlos?"

"I can't tell. I'm going out to see."

Samantha gripped Brock's arm as he was straightening. "Don't leave the cabin. Don't leave me."

He cupped her face. "I have to know, Samantha. I won't be gone long. Lock the door behind me."

"A lock won't stop Carlos."

"But it might make you feel better."

It didn't make her feel better, she thought as she locked the door behind him and began to pace. Two steps one way, then two steps back. It seemed as if she spent her time either running or waiting, and neither was very good for her nerves.

By the time Brock returned to the cabin, Samantha's clothes were completely dry and her nerves were frayed. She had visualized all kinds of horrible things that had happened to him while he was gone. Her imagination was just too vivid for this kind of waiting.

When she unlocked the door to let him in,

she threw her arms about him and hugged him tightly. "Is it Carlos or his men?"

"No, it's the Brazilian authorities, inspecting boats for turtles."

"Turtles! And you believe it?" Aghast at his naïveté, she pulled back. Maybe his malaria fever had done more damage than she had thought.

A deep chuckle rumbled in Brock's chest. "Yes, because they do. Turtles are an endangered species protected by the government, along with some other animals. It's just that the people along the river don't agree with the law, so the government patrols the river and searches boats occasionally."

"What took you so long?"

"Clothes and dinner." Brock held up a bundle he was carrying, then opened the door to retrieve the food he had gotten. "When we leave the steamer in Manaus, I want us to be disguised as locals as best we can. I have a turban for you to put around that hair of yours. It should help some."

"What's for dinner?" Samantha asked, more interested in the food, its tantalizing aroma wafting through the cabin.

"Fish."

"Just so long as it's not another nut."

"And the good captain also gave us a bottle of *cachaça,* the local liquor. He thought we might be celebrating."

At first Samantha declined a glass of the liquor, mixed with fruit juices, but her thirst overcame her common sense finally, and she poured herself a small drink. It did calm her tattered nerves, so she refilled her glass.

As she sipped her third glass, she knew she was going to regret it in the morning. She wasn't use to drinking, but the fruit juices disguised the liquor's potency. Halfway through the third glass, she realized just how much. She was too relaxed and her guard was completely down, which was extremely dangerous around Brock and his masculine appeal.

When they finished their dinner, Brock placed the food tray outside the cabin door. As he turned back into the room, Samantha moved over on the bunk to allow him enough space to sit next to her. He paused, indecision in his expression.

"I won't bite." She patted the bunk, one part of her astonished at her brazen behavior.

"To discuss business?"

"Hardly. To discuss us." She had heard about vampire bats in the Amazon. Had she been bitten by one and not realized it? Was she turning into something entirely different now that the sun was going down?

He remained standing. "If I come over to the bunk, it won't be to waste our time talking."

She laughed, a light musical sound. "Sir, no

gentleman would take advantage of a woman who's had too much to drink."

In one step he was next to the bunk. "I'm no gentleman, Samantha Prince."

"And I'm perfectly sober, Brock Slader."

"Good. I don't want you to regret this tomorrow."

"I probably will anyway. But I'm tired of fighting my feelings."

Brock sat on the bunk. "We're no good for each other."

"I know. As different as day and night." She turned her body to face him.

"I'm a security risk." He wound his arms about her and drew her close.

"An unemployed wanderer." She combed her fingers through his hair, luxuriating in its rich texture.

"With no retirement plan." He bent forward, his mouth an inch from hers.

"The hell with retirement. That's over thirty years away. It's now that I'm concerned about." Samantha brushed her lips across his, once, then twice, the roughness of his beard in stark contrast to the gentleness of his hands as they rubbed up and down her spine.

He pulled back and framed her face with his work-toughened hands, staring into her eyes for a passion-building moment. She took immense satisfaction in watching him watch her. Her effect on him showed in his eyes, now a bright silver with desire, in the slight flaring of his nostrils as his breathing came faster, in the swift beat of his heart beneath her splayed fingers.

"One last chance to do the sensible thing, Samantha."

"From the very beginning we both knew in our hearts this would happen."

"But fought it in our minds." His voice was a seductive whisper, his words fanning her mouth as he dipped his head slowly toward hers.

Any restraint he had evaporated as his lips moved over hers in a hungry mating that reflected his appetite for her, held in check for days. His mouth was driving in its possession, his tongue probing her sweetness, his sensual thrusts firing her senses to a feverish pitch.

Carefully he removed the pins from her hair and ran his fingers through the lush waves, then arranged it about her face in a fiery cloud that enhanced the delicate structure of her features. Again he stared at her beauty. She was so much like the orchid, frail looking but sturdy, surviving in an environment that was harsh even on the people who had lived in it all their lives.

He rubbed his thumb across her kiss-swollen lips and she bit down on its tip, then sucked. He could no longer ignore the silent message in her eyes. It made him feel as though there was no other man in the world for her. It made him feel heady, powerful, but vulnerable too.

She caressed his shoulders and pulled him back to her, her mouth flowering open for him. The continual interplay of their mouths and hands created a deep need in Samantha, a need only Brock could satisfy.

Suddenly the clothes between them were a barrier. Brock worked the buttons of her shirt loose while she unfastened his, their gazes bound as though neither wanted to let go for a moment.

Samantha slid Brock's shirt off his shoulders and down his arms, reveling in the muscles her fingertips discovered along the way. She wanted to go back and explore every crevice, but her breath caught as he leisurely, caressingly, began to remove her shirt, then her bra.

He lowered his head to the pulse at her throat, and his tongue flicked over her heated flesh, teasing her with its delicate whispers. Then he dropped his head even lower to pay homage first to one breast and then the other.

Clutching his shoulders, Samantha threw back her head, her eyes closed. His erotic touches were driving her wild with yearning. Her nipples hardened under his mastery, her skin quivering, burning.

When his mouth returned to coax her lips apart, she responded with uninhibited delight. The intimate fencing of their tongues caused her body to tremble, and Samantha knew in that moment that she never wanted to let go, never wanted to be without Brock's arms about her.

His hand slipped down over her breast to her waist, where he unsnapped her pants and slid the zipper down. Pushing the material apart, he ran his finger along the waistband of her underwear. At the same time he eased her back onto the bunk, positioning her soft contours tantalizingly close to the muscular planes of his body.

Reluctantly he shifted his body, tucking her against him while he swept the rest of her clothes down her legs and onto the floor. His quickly followed, and they were both naked. Brock's hands took and gave pleasure as they roamed over her.

The growing darkness kept Samantha from seeing his expression, but she could imagine the warmth in his eyes, the passion in his features that matched hers. It was conveyed in his every touch, kiss, whisper.

He covered her with his powerful body, parting her legs with his knee, lacing his hands through her hair to hold her head while he rained tiny kisses over her face. Then his mouth fastened onto hers for a long, intoxicating kiss while he plunged inside her. Rhythmically they moved together as one, slowly at first, then faster as their desire grew, burst forth, and knew no boundaries.

She felt his final, sweet surge as wave after wave of delight racked her body, pushing her to the very limits of ecstasy.

Afterward, as he held her cradled against him, she thought: *I belong to this man.*

She could no longer deny the feelings that had begun the first day in the lobby of the Grand Hotel. She nestled even closer to his warm strength, sleep inching over her as the afterglow of their lovemaking dimmed with reality.

She loved a man who wanted no one in his life permanently.

She loved a man who had given up all commitments.

CHAPTER THIRTEEN

"No, I'm going in there with you. We're a team, remember?" Samantha and Brock were seated at a table in the restaurant across from the Grand Hotel.

"Not in this, Samantha." Brock took a sip of his Brazilian coffee, the expression on his face unyielding. "I go alone."

She had expected to hear him say those words when this was all over, but not yet. "You're asking me to sit here and wait for you."

"Yes," he said, his voice firm.

"I've had my fill of waiting, especially after that episode with the Brazilian authorities on the riverboat."

"I don't care. It's safer this way."

"Not on my nerves, which have been stretched, tattered, and pulled apart." She reached across the small table and grasped his hand. "Please, Brock. If they are waiting in there for you—"

"I don't want you in the middle. I can take

care of myself, but if I have to worry about you too . . ." He laid his hand over their clasped ones. "Samantha, I don't want anything to happen to you. I'll go in and scout the place out. I'll get our luggage from the clerk and see if your brother has been there. Then I'll leave. Simple and quick. I'll be back before you know it."

"If Carlos or his men aren't there." If they were, she might never see him again.

"And if they are, what could you do?"

One corner of her mouth lifted. "Scream?"

Brock looked at her hard for a moment, then started chuckling. "That ought to confuse everyone so we could make our getaway."

"You see? I do have some value."

"To me, yes. But only alive and in one piece, Samantha." His voice was husky and his expression softened as his gaze traveled slowly, caressingly, over her features.

Samantha blushed, remembering the past few days on the riverboat. It hadn't been difficult finding something to occupy their time. For a while she had forgotten the trouble they were in; the only thing that had existed for her was Brock and the cabin. He had made her feel every inch a woman, even after traveling in the hot, humid jungle for over a week.

"Besides, even Carlos would have a hard time recognizing me." Brock ran his hand down his jaw.

Samantha had to admit that he did fit right in

with the rest of the people in Manaus. He had let his beard grow out, which was an effective disguise, altering his appearance quite a bit. And with his straw hat pulled down low over his head and the old, worn-looking clothes he had on, Samantha knew it would be difficult for Carlos or Paul to spot him. But she still felt uneasy. What if they did?

"Stay here and guard the black book, Samantha. That's what Carlos really wants anyway. If you come and Carlos is there, he'll have it. This way if I were caught, I'd have some bargaining power."

She couldn't argue with his logic. Frowning, she dropped her gaze to their hands, still clasped on the table. "Don't take any chances." Because she would die if anything happened to him, she silently added.

"I won't. I want to stay in one piece, so there will be no heroics."

"If anyone suspicious is there, turn around and leave. My luggage isn't that important, and there's certainly nothing important in Mark's. Besides, I doubt Mark has returned to the Grand Hotel."

"But I need my luggage. I have all my papers in it."

She reestablished eye contact with him. There was so much she wanted to say before he left, because one part of her was afraid she would never see him again. But the words lodged in her throat. He didn't want ties or a commitment, and her love for him would be one in his eyes. Instead, she squeezed his hand and smiled up at him as he rose to leave.

As she watched him walk from the restaurant, tears misted her eyes. Her eyes closed; she refused to think the worst would happen to him. They had made it this far. They would make it to the end.

For five minutes she sat at the table, absently fingering the fork. She tried to think of something that had nothing to do with what Brock was doing in the Grand Hotel. She couldn't. If anything happened to him, she didn't know what she would do.

Impatient, frustrated, she stood and walked to the window that overlooked the street. The Grand Hotel was across from the restaurant, which afforded Samantha a good view of the entrance.

She positioned herself where no one could see her from the street and waited, watching for any suspicious-looking characters entering the hotel. The problem was, the Grand Hotel being what it was, there were a lot of suspicious-looking people going into the place.

One man in particular caught her full attention, and she tensed, watching him carefully as he made his way into the hotel. There was something familiar about the man that sent an alarm signal off in her brain. Without thinking of the consequences she headed for the door. She had to warn Brock that one of the men who had guarded the plane at the mission was in the Grand Hotel.

She prayed her Brazilian disguise would fool the man from the mission. She was wearing a white cotton skirt and blouse with a white turban on her head to cover her distinctive hair. Brock had darkened her skin even more than the tropical sun had with some concoction he had learned about in the jungle.

When she had caught sight of herself in a store window on the way into the restaurant, she'd had to acknowledge she looked different from the woman who had arrived in Manaus two weeks before. But the most important thing was that she really was a different woman in her heart and mind.

In the lobby entrance she quickly scanned the faces, hoping to see Brock before Carlos's man did. She found Brock at the desk talking with the clerk, their luggage at Brock's feet.

She started forward when she spied the man from the mission. He approached Brock and said something. Samantha ducked behind a large potted plant, the hotel's one concession to decorating the lobby. She watched as Brock and the man exchanged words. A chill of fear encased her like a cold shroud.

Brock was wearing a disguise, but did the man from the mission know it was Brock?

What in the world were they talking about? Why was it taking so long? One question followed another in Samantha's mind before she could find answers to any of them.

She twisted her hands together, her palms sweaty. Her doubts that Brock was working for Carlos resurfaced as the two men continued to talk as if they were friends who had just run into each other. Brock gestured toward the entrance and continued to talk to the man from the mission. Was he telling the man where to find her? Had Brock struck a bargain with Carlos after all?

No, it couldn't be true, she argued with herself. Not after what happened between them on the riverboat. She turned away from the scene, desperately wanting to deny what she had observed.

Clutching her bag, she escaped out to the street and looked around, undecided what to do next. For a long moment, her heart pounding against her chest, she stared at the restaurant. She couldn't go back there.

Where could she go? She didn't know Manaus at all. Whatever she did, she had to do it quickly. She looked around frantically, finally spying a place where she could hide and watch the street in front of the hotel.

She hurried to the alleyway, then tried to act Brazilian and a part of the scenery while she waited for Brock or the man to appear. Brock was the first one to leave the hotel. As he headed across the street to the restaurant, he continually glanced about him, alert, wary.

When he disappeared into the restaurant, Samantha wiped the sweat from her forehead with the back of her hand. Was he going into the restaurant to deliver her personally to Carlos? Or was her vivid imagination taking off again? It was hard for her to deny the friendly exchange between Brock and the guard at the mission, and yet in her heart she knew Brock couldn't turn her over to Carlos after their weeks together.

Not two minutes later Brock reappeared, searching the street, a worried look on his face. Samantha had started to leave her hiding place, berating herself for jumping to conclusions, when the guard appeared in the hotel entrance. She ducked farther behind the building wall, her heartbeat thundering in her ears and drowning out all street sounds.

As Brock moved down the street away from her, she saw the guard leave the hotel and follow Brock. Samantha followed both of them, keeping well back from the pair. She felt as if she were playing in a James Bond movie, but at the moment she couldn't approach either man until she figured out what was going on.

When Brock turned down a narrow street, the man did also. Samantha cautiously peered around the corner and saw that the street was a dead end. Brock was cornered by the guard, who was holding a gun on him. The weapon gleamed in the afternoon sun and sent her heartbeat accelerating at an even faster tempo.

She looked down the main street but couldn't see a policeman. She was quickly scanning the people along the street, trying to decide whom to ask for help, when she realized she couldn't speak the language. She had to be the one to do something.

Next to her feet was a slab of wood. She picked it up and with a tight grip tested its weight. When she entered the dead-end street, the guard was waving the gun at Brock and saying something excitedly. Brock's gaze briefly brushed her before returning to the guard. Brock spoke to the man in a calm, even voice that amazed Samantha. She would have been beside herself if someone were pointing a gun at her.

Step by quiet step she sneaked up on the guard, raising the piece of wood high above her head. She was sure the man could hear her loud heartbeat, but Brock kept his full attention.

With all her strength she swung the wood down onto the man's head, wincing when she heard the thud as she struck him. He crumpled to the ground, and she sagged with relief. She took one look at Brock and ran into his arms, hugging him, checking to make sure he was all right.

"Let's get out of here before we have company."

As they passed the man, Brock bent down and checked his pulse.

"Is—is he alive?" Samantha asked shakily.

"Yes. He'll have a nasty headache, but that's all."

Again she trembled with relief. She would have done it all over again to save Brock, but she hadn't wanted to kill the man, even if he did work for Carlos.

Out in the main street they quickly fled the scene, heading away from the Grand Hotel. Samantha was completely turned around by the time Brock stopped in front of another second-rate hotel.

"We'll stay here for the night and decide how to find your brother."

Brock handled the arrangements, getting a room for them on the second floor with a window overlooking the street below.

After inspecting their room, he turned to her and asked, "Where the hell were you earlier?"

Anger contorted his features and made Samantha step back. "I—" How could she explain that for a while she hadn't trusted him? Somehow she suspected he wouldn't laugh as he had in the jungle.

He covered the distance between them, his

eyes hard, assessing. "Why weren't you in the restaurant?"

She swallowed several times and tried to speak, but nothing would come out.

He gripped her arms and pulled her against him. "You scared me to death. I'd thought for sure that Carlos had you. I could hardly see or think straight when I came out of the restaurant."

"I couldn't wait at the table, so I stood at the window. That's when I saw the guard going into the hotel. I had to warn you."

"I told you I could take care of myself. I have for thirty-eight years."

Her anger began to surface. "And what would you have done if I hadn't come along in the alley?"

"I nearly had him convinced I wasn't the man he was looking for."

Her forehead creased with a frown. "What do you mean?"

"In the hotel lobby he approached me for directions. I knew who he was and that he didn't really want those directions. He was testing me. I guess he wasn't totally convinced I wasn't the man with the American lady, so he followed me. If I hadn't been so worried about you, I wouldn't have turned down a dead-end street."

"Oh, so this is my fault?"

"Absolutely. If you had stayed put, it wouldn't have happened."

"Yeah, instead he would have had both of us at gunpoint."

"Why didn't you come up to me when I came out of the hotel?"

Samantha couldn't look him directly in the eye. "I—I saw the guard following you."

"I don't buy that."

"Why? It's true."

"The guard didn't immediately follow me. I made sure of that before I left."

"Okay." She pulled herself from his grip and put as much distance as possible between them in the small room, pushing back the curtain to gaze out on the street below. "I saw you and the guard together in the lobby. It sure looked as though you two were long-lost buddies." She glanced at Brock, her breath suspended.

"I see. You still think I'm working for Carlos —or at the very least trying to make my own deal." His expression was totally closed, but his voice was full of disgust.

She spun about and faced him. "Oh, no. I don't now. I don't think I ever really did, even on the river."

"You've read too many spy novels."

"You're the one who said we can't trust anyone."

"I didn't mean each other."

"I'm sorry, Brock. It isn't what—"

"I think it's a little late to be sorry." He turned his back on her and opened his suitcase.

"I know you have a perfect right to be angry with me, but under the circumstances—"

"You're wrong, Sam. I'm not angry with you. I'm just disappointed."

The edge to his words made her feel cold in the heat of the tropical city. "Please understand."

"Understand what? We owe each other nothing, Sam. This is a business arrangement between us, no more. You made that perfectly clear from the beginning."

"But on the riverboat—"

"That was a nice way to pass a few days that otherwise would have been boring."

"So I'm just a diversion from boredom?"

"I'm staying for one thing only: my ten percent of whatever your brother is talking about. I just hope I'm not being played for a fool. Now, don't you think we should get back to the business at hand of finding your brother and solving the mystery of the book?"

"Oh, by all means. I wouldn't want you to be cheated out of your percentage. We both need to get on with our *normal* lives."

Outwardly she appeared quietly angry, but inside she was hurting. By misjudging him she had lost any chance of ever making a relationship between them last. Part of her understood and felt his anger was justified, but why couldn't he understand that the strange adventure she had been thrust into was often overwhelming and frightening? Logically his behavior at the hotel had been questionable, and her survival instinct had prompted her evasive action. In her heart, emotionally, she had known he wasn't capable of betraying her like that.

"The book, Sam? We'll need it if we're going to decipher the code. That is, if you trust me enough to look at it."

Clenching her teeth, she delved into her bag and produced the black book.

Brock flipped through the pages, his forehead wrinkling with a frown of concentration. Finally he handed it back to Samantha. "Any ideas?"

As she examined the book, she said, "I can't shake the feeling that I should know this code. But numbers and letters? It doesn't make sense."

"Codes rarely do except to the people who use them. Let's start with the obvious and work from there."

"I read a book once—"

"Only once?"

She glared at him and continued, "About a code someone devised involving starting in the middle of the alphabet with *M* and alternating letters and numbers." She wrote the beginning of the code down to show him.

"Maybe your brother read the same book. Let's see what we get." Brock sat at the table that rocked every time he moved his hand across the pad. When he was through deciphering the first sentence of the message, he slid the paper across the table so Samantha could see it. "Unless this is a new language, I would say it's probably not the right code."

They began going through possibilities, some wild ones, but after working on the book for three hours, all they had produced was a floor littered with discarded paper. They had ceased even the semblance of working together the last hour and each had his own pad, trying to break the code before the other.

Samantha had a hard time concentrating on the jumbled letters and numbers of Mark's book. Every time Brock moved, her attention was drawn to him—against her will, she told herself, knowing it was a lie. She loved the way his brow knitted and his jaw tensed when he was in deep thought.

Samantha was watching Brock scribble some letters on the paper when he suddenly stopped writing in midword. Her gaze slowly, almost reluctantly, traveled up to his face. His eyes sparkled with silent humor as he stared at her staring at him.

"Come up with anything?" she asked, her voice breathless, betraying her reaction to his blatant sex appeal.

"Yes . . ."

"You did?"

He smiled, slowly and definitely with mischief. "Yeah. That I'm tired of looking at numbers and letters and that I'm hungry. What about you?"

"Do you think it's safe to go out?"

"What do you suggest we do?"

Her secret suggestion would have had nothing to do with eating. She vividly recalled the way they had sated their appetites on the riverboat. Finally, because he was expecting her to answer, she said, "One of us can go out and bring some food back while the other guards the book."

"Any orders?"

One of her eyebrows rose. "You're assuming I don't want to go."

His smile broadened. "I'm not assuming anything, Sam. It's very simple. I'm going because I speak the language and can order the food."

"You're more familiar with Brazilian food, so anything that's edible will be fine with me." She was exhausted, too, with trying to decode the book and match wits with Brock. Above anything else, she really wanted to be held, loved, and told everything would work out.

He put on his straw hat and left. While he was gone, Samantha stared at the book, the letters and numbers blending together. A childhood memory flitted in and out of her mind, trying to take shape. . . .

"Come on, Sam. It'll be fun making up our own code." Mark's boyish face lit with a smile. "We can play spy. I've got a great idea. I'll use your name."

"My name? What are you talking about, Mark?"

"Your name will be numbers, then the rest of the alphabet will be letters starting at the end and working to the front. Come on, Sam, let's write a secret message."

Samantha blinked, seeing again the aged hotel room.

That was it! Mark's code was the same one he'd used when he was eight.

She straightened in the chair and began to translate. By the time Brock returned to the room with the food, she knew what Mark had written.

Before Brock had closed the door completely, Samantha was across the room and throwing her arms about his neck.

"We're rich! It's gold!"

CHAPTER FOURTEEN

"It isn't a city of gold but a large deposit of it. The book has very detailed directions to its location," Samantha exclaimed while she relished the feel of Brock's arms about her.

"You're kidding!" He pulled back to look her in the eye.

"I'd never kid about something like gold. We'll all be rich!" Her smile encompassed her whole face.

He picked her up and swung her around and around, laughing from the sheer excitement of her discovery. Then suddenly he stopped; their gazes touched, his laughter died, her smile faded.

"Samantha," he whispered, then slowly brought his mouth down to hers. His mouth hungrily devoured hers, his tongue parting her lips to slip between her teeth, darting in and out in sensual caresses.

"Oh, Brock, I'm so sorry I ever doubted you. Please love me."

He tensed and straightened, then put her back on the floor and stepped away.

Samantha was both angry and unsatisfied. "Just for a moment you were able to forget your anger and react to me the way you really want to, like you did on the steamer." She spoke to his back, which was a rigid wall, shielding her from his expression. "I made a mistake. I'm human. Can you stand there and tell me you've never made a mistake in your life, Brock Slader?"

He pivoted, his gray eyes sharp, cutting. "I've made my share of mistakes. One was helping a woman in a hotel lobby."

She met his hard gaze with one of her own. "You'll get paid for your services."

"All of them?" His one raised brow mocked her.

Samantha's eyes widened. For a few seconds she was numbed by his remark. Then the pain came, and she had a difficult time fighting back the tears. She spun around, biting her lower lip to hold back her emotions that were cart-wheeling between rage and anguish.

When he touched her shoulder, she flinched and put as much space between them as possible in the small room. She gazed out the window down onto the darkened street below, not really seeing anything.

"I didn't mean that, Samantha. I'm the one who should say I'm sorry."

"Why?" She tried to sound as though his words hadn't hurt, but she heard her voice quaver.

"Because I wanted to hurt you like you had hurt me."

She faced him. "I didn't think you were capable of feeling that particular emotion."

"I've tried my damndest not to care about you, but I do, Samantha."

"Samantha?"

"You seem more like a Samantha to me now than a Sam."

"Prim, proper, formal?"

"No. Feminine, soft, very beautiful. I wanted to forget the days we spent on the riverboat. I can't. I seized the opportunity this afternoon to use anger to force me to forget what we shared. It didn't work, Samantha."

"You're not angry or disappointed that for a few minutes today I wasn't sure I could trust you."

"I won't deny it didn't hurt or disappoint me, but I can understand why you felt that way. We've both been thrust into an unusual situation. We haven't known each other long."

"My normal, ordinary world has been turned upside down. I sometimes feel I'm meeting myself coming and going. I've never imagined myself having to run for my life."

He chuckled. "Not even briefly when you've read an adventure or a spy thriller?"

"Not even briefly."

He crossed the room to her. "I thought you immersed yourself into the characters of the books you read."

"It's one thing to go through an adventure with some characters on a printed page and a completely different thing to actually live an adventure."

He rubbed his hands up and down her arms. "You realize how high the stakes are?"

She nodded.

"The mere mention of gold drives men to do things that in normal circumstances they wouldn't even think of doing."

The molten silver of his eyes mesmerized her. "Our lives as well as Mark's are on the line."

"I'm afraid it's us or Carlos."

She couldn't look away from the fiery claim in his eyes. "Hold me, Brock."

He took her into his arms as if it were the most natural thing in the world. They felt so right around Samantha that she didn't know how she would cope when she had to leave him. In two weeks time he had entrenched himself into her life until she didn't think she could live without him.

His arms about her were a sheath of gentleness as he whispered against the top of her head, "We're two people set in our ways, Samantha. Stubborn, full of pride. Neither wants to give in. Both of us are afraid and wary of the emotions we're feeling. Let's settle on taking each day we have together as it comes and enjoy whatever time has been granted us."

"But in the end we go our separate ways?" She wasn't sure she wanted to hear his answer, the only one she knew he would give.

"Is there any other way for us? I could never punch a time clock again. I've tried your world. I can't live in it."

"You are assuming again. What if I could live in your world?"

"From the very beginning I've made it clear that long-term commitments aren't in my life plan."

"I thought you didn't plan." With her arms tightening about him and her head against his chest, she squeezed her eyes closed and tried to imagine what it would be like without Brock; she couldn't. And yet, she wasn't ready to give up her life to wander the world. It went against everything she believed in and had always thought she wanted. "You are right about me. I couldn't see myself living from day to day with no regard for the future. It's not me, but it is you."

He tilted up her head so he could kiss her, his tongue invading the heated moistness of her mouth. She felt the burning seal of his kiss deep in her soul and decided she would cherish every precious moment she had with him. When the time came, she would deal with the pain of parting.

His tongue slowly, sensuously, traced the outline of her mouth before he kissed each corner, saying, "You have been a breath of spring in my life."

Savoring the tingling pressure of his mouth on hers, she wondered when they went their separate ways if her life would be colder than winter in the Arctic. She never did like cold weather. Would she ever feel this kind of warmth again? For once she wasn't going to think of the future but live for the moment.

Samantha gave him free access to her slender neck while her hands explored the planes of his back and shoulders. How well he blended with the wildness of the jungle. He was daring and bold, as unconquerable as the Amazon they had traveled through.

His mouth and tongue teased the sensitive flesh of her throat, and soon she felt her knees buckling under the enticement of his loving. She gripped him for support, swaying into his strength.

He lifted his head and their gazes met, reflecting their need for each other. Brock raised her hand to his mouth and sucked on her fingers, taking one between his teeth to bite, the gentle savagery of the action in contradiction to the tenderness in his eyes. But it emphasized how contradictory his presence was in her orderly life.

She nuzzled her cheek into the palm of his hand and turned to kiss the roughness with whispering caresses. For breathless moments she became lost in the silvery intensity of his eyes as she nipped each of his fingertips, tasting his salty skin.

Taking deep breaths, her breasts straining against her blouse, she broke visual contact with him, feeling he had read the love she had for him in her eyes. It gave him such power if he chose to use it.

His gaze slid down the length of her to rest on her breasts, her nipples hardening under his ardent attention. He loosened the top button, then the second one, until her blouse parted to reveal her lacy bra.

He reestablished eye contact with her, murmuring, "I don't think I could ever tire of you, Samantha."

"Love me, even if it's for a short time," she said, her husky voice laced with the need to feel the fulfilment only he could give her.

Suddenly they stood back and hurriedly undressed, as if their time together was very limited. They were several feet apart, naked, their gazes greedily sweeping down the length of each other, memorizing every line and curve for the lonely times ahead.

They were fire and air, coming together in a

fiery blaze in every aspect of their relationship; they fought intensely, they loved intensely.

His mouth, that could be demanding, unrelentingly set or tender, opened over hers and gloried in her warmth, in her promise of ecstasy. While his thumbs massaged the sides of her neck in slow, tantalizing circles, he worshiped her with murmured words and a deep kiss that sought to heighten the passion already between them.

The soft glow of moonlight that streamed through the partially opened curtains illuminated his body, accentuating his powerful, lean frame as Brock carried Samantha to the bed and gently deposited her in the middle, then quickly joined her. He exploited every sensitive place she had to the fullest with his mouth and hands until she felt feverish with her aching need.

She in turn used her knowledge of him to drive him to the brink of insanity, needing to give him pleasure. She wanted to leave her mark on him forever. She didn't want him to forget her or this time they had together, however brief in the scope of their lives.

Their new certainty of each other intensified the wondrous quality of their lovemaking, and when Samantha felt she could wait no longer, she pulled Brock to her and whispered, "Now!"

He poised above her, with a hand on each side of her head, and stared down at her for a timeless moment. Then his mouth met hers with a crushing force. Their joining was a combustive welding that rocked them both.

As they lay in each other's arms, Samantha wanted to tell Brock she loved him. Yet he would see it as a chain she was trying to place about him, so she remained quiet, waiting for him to break the silence.

"Samantha, I wish I was different, but . . ." His voice trailed off. He knew he didn't have to complete the sentence. They both knew he wouldn't, couldn't, change.

The bittersweet longing in his voice made her heart twist with the impossibility of their situation. She was realistic enough to realize that love didn't conquer everything, no matter how much a person wished it could.

"You can't teach an old dog new tricks," she said with as much lightness as she could muster.

The silence lengthened between them as Brock pulled her even closer.

"Tomorrow we have to begin looking for your brother."

"How? You said if a man wants to get lost in this town he can."

"Let's hope he wants to get in contact with you. After all, you have the book now."

"What if he's at the gold mine?"

"Maybe he needs the directions as much as Carlos."

"I can call Nell at my store in New Orleans. Mark may have tried calling me there."

"That's a place to start. We'll see what she has to say." He rolled over onto his side, facing her. "You realize this is the first time we've slept in the almost comforts of home in days."

Samantha laughed. "Yeah, that bunk on the riverboat was a bit crowded."

"I didn't hear any complaints at the time."

She knew by his tone of voice that amusement was dancing in his silver-gray eyes. "Who said I didn't like a crowd?"

He chuckled, deep in his throat, a purely sensual sound that stirred Samantha's senses.

"Let me amend what I said. Who said I didn't like things a bit crowded?"

"I think you'd better stop before you dig yourself into a deep hole."

"Would you save me again?"

"Isn't that the duty of a knight?"

"But you don't rescue damsels in distress."

"I can be persuaded by a beautiful face."

"Ah, so it's only my beautiful face that turns you on."

"That and your beautiful body, your beautiful mind, your beautiful—"

Laughing, Samantha fastened her mouth to his and forced him back onto the bed, trapping him with her arms and body.

"We should get some sleep," he whispered against her cheek.

"Yes," she murmured, then continued to trail kisses to his earlobe.

"We should get up early and—"

Her mouth bit lovingly on the shell of his ear; her tongue outlined it.

"The hell with what we should do. I was never one for doing the sensible thing."

"Nell, can you hear me?" Samantha asked in a loud whisper. She was in the hotel lobby and didn't want to raise her voice anymore than that, though there was static on the line.

"Yes. Where have you been? I've been frantic. I haven't heard from you for almost two weeks and you said you would check in every few days." Nell's rush of words was anything but soft.

Samantha smiled, picturing the concerned impatience on her friend's face and knowing that she would have felt the same way if Nell had gone off on some crazy hunt with no warning. "Hold on and I'll explain."

"Well, it isn't like you not to check in when you said you would. I was about to check with the authorities in Brazil. I was scared to death that something had happened to you too."

Samantha tensed. "Happened to me too? Did you hear something about Mark?" She felt Brock's hand settle on her shoulder in silent support. As he kneaded her coiled muscles, she

251

leaned back into him, bracing herself for the worse.

"No, nothing bad. You went to Brazil because he had disappeared and then when you did, too, I naturally became worried."

"I'm fine," Samantha assured her friend, her eyes closing in relief for a few seconds.

"You did have a long distance call a few days back, but the man didn't leave his name."

Samantha felt sure it was her brother. "I haven't found Mark yet. That may have been him. I want to let you know where I'm staying now."

"I know you aren't at the Grand Hotel because I've tried several times. That desk clerk is very uncooperative."

Samantha laughed, thinking of her dealings with the man. She gave Nell the name of the new hotel. "If Mark calls back, tell him it's extremely important that he contact me here under the name of Brock Slader, but under no circumstances, Nell, tell anyone else where I'm staying. No one. Not even the police."

"Police? Oh, my gosh, what have you gotten yourself into, Samantha?"

"I'm not running from the police, Nell," Samantha said in amusement, knowing the shocked expression that must be on Nell's face at that moment. "But I don't know who to trust and you can't be sure it's really the police."

"How will I know it's your brother calling?"

By mentioning the code Samantha knew her brother would realize she had the book and knew what he had discovered. "Ask him about the code he devised as a child. Mark will remember that." The static on the long distance connection was growing louder. "Do you understand?"

"Yes. Will you be calling back?"

"Tomorrow. That's a promise." As her gaze automatically scanned the lobby of the hotel, Samantha hoped she would be able to keep her promise.

"Are you sure you're fine? You sound like you're in trouble. Who's this Brock Slader?"

My lover, my rescuer. "Someone helping me to find Mark." Even if Brock hadn't been standing behind her, she wasn't ready to put into words everything that he meant to her. "I've got to go, Nell."

Samantha's hand remained on the receiver even after she hung up the phone. Nell reminded her of everything back in New Orleans that she had once taken for granted. Hearing her friend's voice made Samantha long for this to be over and everyone to be safe.

But at the same time she realized her life would never be the way it was, not after Brock. She wanted Brock *and* her life in New Orleans, and she knew she couldn't have both. She sighed with resignation.

Brock turned her to face him, his arms

loosely entwined about her, bringing her close against him. "Are you all right?"

"I'm fine." She raised her eyes and saw the concern in his. "No, I'm not, Brock. What do we do next? Mark may never call New Orleans again."

"Let's give it a day or two before I start combing the city."

"I?"

"Yes, Samantha. Just me. You'll remain here with the book. And this time you'd better not follow me. I can take care of myself if I'm not worrying about you."

"And I can take care of myself, especially if I don't have to wait worrying about you. I'm no good at rescuing knights in distress."

He held her close. "Oh, I'd say you're very good. But I'm going this one alone, Samantha. No arguing."

She toyed with the top button of his shirt, looking up at him through lowered lashes. "Can we continue this discussion in our room?"

He brushed her hand away, laughter in his eyes. "No. If Carlos's men are looking for us, it will be easier to spot us together. Alone I can cover more ground."

"Are you implying I'm excess baggage?"

"I know I'm going to regret saying this," Brock looked heavenward, "but in this case, yes, you are."

"You say I have a day to convince you otherwise."

Shaking his head, he replied, "I'm banking on the fact that your brother will call and this subject will be academic."

Samantha sauntered toward the stairs, her mind already going over strategies to use in convincing Brock that she should go with him to look for Mark. A smile graced her lips as Brock unlocked their door. He knew the language, but she knew what Mark looked like.

Brock tossed the key onto the dresser, then walked to the window to check the street below. When he turned around, he asked, "Do you have any cards?"

"Yes. Why?"

"Well, for the next twenty-four hours we're going to be holed up in here. I thought we would play something."

Her eyes gleamed. "Play? What, sir?"

"Strip poker?"

"That sounds delicious." She opened her suitcase and placed the deck on the bed. "Deal."

CHAPTER FIFTEEN

"Okay, I want to know who taught you to play poker so well," Brock demanded while unbuttoning his shirt.

Samantha's laughter filled the room. "My brother. He's quite good. In fact, he's considered a card shark."

"Is his sister?" he grumbled as he leisurely slipped his shirt off his shoulders and shrugged out of it, the playful gleam in his eyes contrasting with his rough voice.

"Why, Mr. Slader! Me, a card shark?" She looked properly offended while she took his shirt and laid it on the pile of his clothes that she had already acquired. "Do you want a rematch?" As she shuffled the deck, she added, "That could be your sixth loss. Or would you rather admit defeat?"

"I don't think my ego can take losing six times in a row. Why don't we forget all the preliminaries"—he winked, smiling roguishly—"and get right down to business?"

"We've already deciphered the book," she commented innocently, and started a game of solitaire on the bed. "I have another deck of cards somewhere in my suitcase if you want to play double solitaire."

His chuckle was full of male arrogance, as well as his look. "You've got the right words, *to play*, but the wrong game, lady."

"Oh, and what game do you have in mind?"

"Something a bit more athletic than cards."

"I'm not very good in sports, so I don't go out for them much. I'd better—sit this one out." She resisted the urge to bat her eyelashes and instead smiled sweetly while she continued playing solitaire.

His sensuous gaze caught her mischievous one. "In this sport you are definitely good." With one sweep of his arm he cleared the bed of cards and tugged her toward him. "But, as with any sport, in order to become better, you must practice."

"And practice," she murmured against his lips.

She circled her arms around his neck and kissed him hard on the mouth, not giving him time to say anything.

Together, they fell backward and rolled over until they both were lying on the bed, Brock on top, his leg thrown over Samantha's while he pinned her wrists to the mattress above her head. Silent laughter, mingling with desire, danced in his eyes.

"We may be here hours going over the same maneuvers," he whispered into her ear. His voice, strained with passion, tickled her cheek.

"What maneuvers are we going to cover?"

"More like uncover. For instance, you have too much on here." He slipped his hand under her T-shirt and brought the cotton material up and over her head. "Ah, that's better," he rasped, swallowing convulsively as his gaze drank in the magnificent sight of her, half naked, her eyes filled with desire.

"Is that all?" she asked breathlessly, running her tongue suggestively over her slightly parted lips.

He blinked, glanced back at her face, and seemed to mentally shake himself before continuing, "Now, let's see." His gaze covetously roved down the length of her. "We definitely need to remove these." He slid down the zipper on her pants and quickly took them off, leaving her with only her underpants on. His finger traced the waistband, then trailed across her flat stomach to draw a circle around her breast.

"If you ever get tired of wandering the earth, there's a dress store next to my shop that could use you to undress mannequins," she teased, rubbing her body against his.

The ardent light in his eyes dimmed; his

hands stopped caressing her. "Sam, I won't get tired."

"Can you be so sure of the future? I thought you didn't go in for making plans of any sort." For twenty-four hours they had been avoiding the subject of their future together—or rather the nonexistence of a future together.

"There are some things I know about myself. I don't kid myself either."

"And you think I do?"

He nodded, twisted away, and stood. Retrieving his pants from the pile of clothes, he stepped into them. "Maybe you should call Nell. Then I'll go out to check around for your brother."

"The sooner we find my brother, the sooner I'm on my way back to the States? Is that your plan?" Sarcasm laced her voice as she sat up, holding the sheet to her chest as if it were a shield.

"Yes, dammit!" He gathered up her clothes and tossed them to her. "Get dressed."

His closed expression was back, and Samantha wanted to scream with frustration. Damn him! "Why are you suddenly shutting me out? We've come too far in our relationship to go backward now."

He tucked his shirt into his pants, then sat on the bed to put on his shoes and socks. Tension knotted the muscles of his back and shoulders as he continued dressing with jerky movements. "Because I realize this whole thing was a mistake."

"Making love?"

"Yes."

"How can you say that?" Her anger began to take hold.

"You're dreaming that we can have a life together."

"Can you deny the excitement and pleasure we've shared these last few days?"

"No, I won't. But it's not reality. You want to extend the fantasy beyond Brazil, and I know it wouldn't work between us. You have me painted into a picture with you in New Orleans, living in suburbia, commuting to work five days a week. Does the house have a white picket fence around it? How many children do we have in your dream?"

"Don't flatter yourself." Samantha scrambled from the bed and quickly donned her clothes, her pain and anger blotting out the panicky edge in Brock's voice.

"This"—she swept her arm wide to indicate the rumpled bed—"was a nice way to spend some time waiting. I told you I wasn't very good at waiting. I must commend you on your ability to make the time go by so fast. You are very entertaining. I—" She suddenly stopped and drew in a deep, calming breath. Through shimmering eyes she watched Brock cross the room to her, anguish in his eyes.

Drawing her into his embrace, he whispered in a raw voice, "Samantha, I never wanted to hurt you. I think I'm handling this all wrong. I've handled this whole situation wrong from the very beginning. I should never have taken you to the mission. I should have walked away from the scene in the hotel lobby."

She inhaled another deep breath and pulled away from him, making sure none of the hurt showed on her expression. "I'm fine. Really. I think we'd better call Nell, then look for Mark if we have to."

His eyebrows rose. "We?"

"We're a team. We're in this together. Yes, we," she said firmly, placing some distance between them while she finished dressing.

She was determined to put their relationship back on a bantering level, nonpersonal, all business. She had to if she was going to leave Manaus with her dignity and pride intact. Brock had made it painfully clear there was no place for her in his life, but it was extremely difficult to remember that when she was so near him.

"I thought we settled this yesterday, Sam. I'll go look for Mark while you stay here and guard the book."

She lifted her chin a fraction. "You may have settled it, but I didn't. I can be very stubborn. Now, I can either go with you at your side, or I

261

will follow you like yesterday. Which will it be?"

With a sigh he rolled his eyes, asking no one in particular, "How did I ever deserve this?"

"Good, I'm glad you see the wisdom in my accompanying you on your search." Samantha walked to the door and waited for Brock.

Downstairs in the lobby Brock placed another long distance call to New Orleans for Samantha. When the phone was ringing at her store, he handed her the receiver.

"Nell, this is Samantha. Has my brother called back?"

"Yes, a few hours after you phoned yesterday. I gave him the message and he said he would contact you. He hasn't?"

"No," Samantha answered slowly, trying to keep her alarm at bay. There could be a lot of reasons why he hadn't contacted her yet. But all the ones she thought of meant he was in trouble and couldn't get to her. "Thanks, Nell. We'll wait here until he does."

"When are you coming home? Everyone is asking about you."

"If I'm lucky, in a couple of days. Bye." Samantha hung up and turned to Brock. "He called the shop yesterday and told Nell he would be in touch with us." Her eyes were round with fear, and her voice held a trace of panic in it.

"Sam, don't jump to any conclusions. He

262

may not even be in Manaus. At least now we know to stay right here until we hear from him."

She forced her body to relax. "Yes, you're right. What do we do now? Wait upstairs in the room?"

"I'll check with the desk. Maybe there's a message for us."

She was glad one of them was thinking straight. Samantha's mind was a maze of jumbled thoughts. It was hard dealing with her emotions concerning Brock and the trouble Mark was in at the same time.

At the desk there was a message and a package for them from Mark. The clerk told Brock that a young boy had delivered them to the hotel that morning. Brock and Samantha decided to wait until they were upstairs in their room before opening it and reading the message.

A man watched them as they headed for the stairs. When they had disappeared from the man's view, he approached the clerk and laid some money on the counter. The man's smile was broad as he left to report the contents of Mark Prince's note to his sister. Tonight the Major would have the directions to the gold and the only other people who knew about it— all three of them. The Major wanted no one left to talk about the large gold discovery.

Meanwhile, upstairs in their hotel room,

Brock and Samantha carefully went over the note from Mark.

"He wants us to go to a carnival ball this evening?" Samantha again examined the note closely to make sure it was her brother's handwriting.

"He'll be there as a joker and he wants you to wear the costume he sent in the package and bring the book."

"Should we? This ball may not be a safe place to exchange something like that."

"I certainly don't want to leave it behind. We'll each take half of the book pages. Since they're small, we can conceal them easily."

"Why a carnival ball with so many people around?"

"I guess your brother feels safer in a crowd of merrymakers. He might be right."

Soon everything would be over with, Samantha thought, and she would be able to return to New Orleans in a day or two. The prospect of seeing Mark again relieved her; the prospect of saying good-bye to Brock depressed her. By the end of the week she would be placing orders for her store and recommending books to her customers. Why wasn't she more excited about returning to her normal, safe life?

The crowd of merrymakers, all dressed in various outlandish costumes, pressed in on Samantha as she scanned the people, trying to find a joker.

"Nothing," she murmured disappointedly, settling back down on her three-inch heels.

She was still astonished at the outfit her brother had sent to her. She wasn't even sure she should call it a costume, it was so scant. She felt definitely underdressed in her harem attire, and she was going to give her brother a piece of her mind when she did catch up with him—after hugging him and making sure he was all right.

"We were early. The ball has just started, Sam."

"I couldn't stand to wait another minute in that hotel room." In truth Samantha couldn't stand to be so near Brock and not be able to tell him she loved him, to touch him, make love to him, and know it would lead to a permanent relationship.

"Give your brother time. He's probably waiting for the ball to get into full swing."

Brock stood next to her, dressed in a pirate's costume. When he had returned to their room and shown it to her, he had said he couldn't pass it up, knowing she would appreciate it.

"What if something has happened to him? What if we can't find him in this crowd? I can't believe he suggested a carnival ball. It's worse than I thought. It's chaos." She tried to keep her voice from sounding frantic, but she didn't think she was doing a very good job.

"I think that's the reason your brother set up this meeting place. It's easy to get lost in a crowd of half-drunk people."

For another fifteen minutes they both looked around for Mark, but when they had seen every costume imaginable but a joker, Brock said, "I'll scout out the garden. I've noticed people going outside. Stay put and I'll be back in a few minutes."

Samantha nodded absently, for her attention was trained on the entrance. Another horde of revelers was coming into the ballroom. In the midst of the new arrivals there was a joker, and Samantha's heart leapt at the sight. When the joker looked her way, she waved at him from across the room and caught his attention. He waved back and motioned for her to follow him.

A mass of people stood between them, and it took quite a while for Samantha to weave her way across the ballroom.

At first she couldn't see Mark; then she spied him near an entrance off the ballroom. Her gaze was fixed on her brother as he disappeared down a hallway, and she followed him as quickly as possible, determined not to lose him.

He went into a room, signaling at the doorway for her to hurry. When she turned the

266

knob, she finally realized that Brock wasn't behind her and that she was completely alone. Brock had the other half of the book.

Well, she'd explain to Mark, then go find Brock, she thought as she stepped into the deserted looking room. Where was Mark?

Bewildered, she was turning around to leave when the lights went out, the door slammed close behind her, and a hand smothered her scream, cutting off her breath. Her lungs started burning as she struggled against the large body, trying to inhale some air. With her legs kicking the shins of the man who held her captive, she bit down hard on the soft flesh of his hand.

"Bitch!" Carlos muttered, but retained a tight hold on her struggling body. "Where's the book? I know your brother gave it to you." He tried to lock her against him while searching her body.

Suddenly the door burst open and the man was pulled away from her, his huge body thrown against the wall. She raced toward the door and the light switch. Flipping it on, she whirled to find Brock pounding his fist into Carlos's jaw. He slumped forward and collapsed to the marble floor.

Samantha was instantly across the room, throwing herself into Brock's arms. "Where the hell have you been?" she asked laughingly between kisses.

"Taking care of Paul in the garden. He followed me outside and jumped me when I was alone."

Samantha pulled back and examined Brock's face. "Are you okay?"

"Fine," he murmured, his mouth slowly descending toward hers. His eyes grew dark with passion. "And you?"

"I'm fine." Her lips whispered across his once, then again. She molded her body into his while her hands explored his back.

"Well, well. What has happened here, Sis? I came to rescue you and everything's been taken care of."

Samantha pivoted to face her brother, who was lounging nonchalantly against the door frame, smiling devilishly. Her hands flew to her waist, and she took several steps toward him, anger and relief fighting for supremacy.

Anger won. "You've come to rescue me! What the hell have you been doing all this time?"

Mark shoved himself away from the door, his grin wiped from his face as he backed away from his angry sister. "My intention at the beginning of this whole mess was to leave Brazil and wait until Carlos got tired of looking for me. But everywhere I turned Carlos or his men were there. I went into hiding. Then I found out from your assistant in New Orleans that you were in Manaus with the book from the mission and I saw an opportunity to set this all up to catch Carlos. I knew until he was captured none of us would be safe."

"You used me and didn't tell me?"

"I couldn't without tipping him off to the trap. Believe me, I didn't want to use you as a pawn, and I certainly didn't like the idea. But, Sam, when you came down here, you put yourself into the middle of a hornet's nest."

"Mark Prince, I should—"

"I'm Brock Slader. I gather you're Samantha's brother," Brock said in amusement as he reached around Samantha to offer Mark his hand.

"Yes. I want to thank you for helping Sam out." Mark shook Brock's hand, looking definitely relieved that Brock had interrupted Samantha's tirade. He'd had enough of them while they were growing up. "These last few weeks have been a nightmare. I was finally able to reach a friend who could arrange this trap."

"Who are these men?" Brock laid a comforting hand on Samantha's shoulder and pulled her back against him.

Mark pointed to Carlos on the floor. "He's a major at a military outpost in the Amazon, so therefore the situation was a delicate one. I had to make sure I solicited the right kind of help. Gold makes men greedy. I had to wait until my friend returned from an assignment in the Amazon."

Behind Mark were three Brazilian policemen, ready to take Carlos into custody. Samantha watched as the major, regained consciousness and the policemen dragged him to his feet and took him out of the room. Obviously Mark's friend was able to arrange the "right" kind of assistance.

"His cohort is in the garden," Brock said.

"He's being taken care of right now." Mark looked from Brock to his sister. "Sam, am I forgiven for getting you into this mess? At the time you were the only one I could turn to for help. I thought I could get out of the country and be in New Orleans to reassure you in person that I hadn't gotten in too deep. As it turned out, things weren't that easy. I underestimated the Major's influence."

When Mark flashed her his smile that he knew she could never resist, her anger melted completely, and only her relief that he was alive and safe remained. "How could I stay mad at you when you added such spice to my life? Just don't do it again."

"You're both entitled to an explanation after I take care of some details with the police. I'll meet you back at your hotel in an hour and retrieve the book then."

After her brother left, the silence was fraught with tension. Everything would be fine with her brother, and now it was time to move on with her life. Samantha didn't want this moment to happen. She squeezed her eyes shut and wished for the impossible.

"Sam?"

Her heart thudded against her chest. Her breath came out raggedly. She knew what Brock was going to say.

He turned her around to face him, and she stared up into his eyes with an appealing look. "Sam, I have to—oh, hell, let's go back to the hotel and wait for your brother. We'll talk later."

They both were postponing the inevitable, but Samantha would take every minute granted her. She nodded, wanting to reach up and cup his face, impelling him to kiss her. Instead, she turned and headed for the door and the hotel—and eventually that talk.

In their hotel room they both paced, avoiding any physical contact. But when she occasionally looked at Brock, she found him looking back at her. Tension gnawed at her nerves until she couldn't stand the silence any longer.

"What are you going to do after Mark arrives?" she asked, stopping in the middle of the room.

He pivoted to face her, his eyes dull. "It depends."

"On what?"

"On your brother."

"Don't worry. You've earned your ten percent. Mark will fulfill the promise I made to you."

"You're very sure of your brother."

"I told you we were very close."

His gaze drilled into her. "It's not the money or the gold I'm concerned about. It's you. I want to make sure he's going to be around." He attempted a smile that didn't quite reach his eyes. "After all, you don't know how to speak the language."

Her heartbeat slowed to a painful throb. "I can take care of myself. If that's all that's keeping you here, then please go. I'll make sure Mark gets your share to you for your oil deal." She held her head at a proud angle, her body rigid.

Brock ran his fingers through his hair repeatedly while his gaze remained linked to hers. "Damn, this isn't easy."

Good, she thought, because it was tearing her up inside. In the back of her mind she had hoped when this moment arrived he would change his mind and return to New Orleans with her. From the beginning there had been a part of her which hadn't accepted that a person would prefer this life to the one she lived.

"It just wouldn't work between us, Sam."

"I see we're back to Sam again." She tried to inject some lightness into her voice.

"We're from two different worlds."

"Oh, do you come from someplace I don't know about?" Her question came out in a strained voice, and she swallowed to ease her dry throat.

In two strides he was in front of her. "Making light of it isn't going to work, Sam. You know what I mean and I believe you agree with me."

With wide, shimmering eyes, she stared up into his endearing face. "Yes, I do agree with you. I can't even stand here and fight with you over it. These past two weeks have been unreal." Finally she reached up and framed his face with her trembling hands. "Wonderful, ecstatic, but not real. My reality is New Orleans and my bookstore. Yours is this place or some other place like it."

He covered her hands with his own. "If I hadn't lived in your world, I'd be sorely tempted to give it a try. But I have, and I know what it would do to me." He twisted his head to kiss the palm of her hand. "Good-bye, Samantha. Tell your brother if he wants to get in touch with me I'll be staying at the Grand Hotel for the next few days."

"Then where?"

He stepped back, holding her hands in his. "Who knows?" For one static moment he looked deep into her eyes. Then he left.

"I love you, Brock Slader," Samantha whispered to the empty room.

CHAPTER SIXTEEN

"What do you think of this one, Samantha?"

"Another trip, Mrs. Carson?" Samantha looked up from arranging some books on the shelf, remembering their conversation two months before and how she had wished she could go away to someplace warm.

"You guessed it." The older woman handed Samantha the book she was thinking of buying.

"Not enough adventure," Samantha immediately replied. "Dull." Like her life lately, she added silently, not really surprised at the admission. In the six weeks since she had returned from the Amazon, she had pretended everything was back to normal, that she was happy and content with her secure life. But she couldn't kid herself. There was nothing normal about pacing her living room every night, wondering what Brock was doing at the moment, or sitting at the store counter staring into space, lost in a dream world of green plants, humidity, and heat.

She had gone into the jungle dependent on Brock; when they had come out of the jungle, they had been dependent on each other. It had been a time for change and growth in a different direction for her, and she hadn't completely realized that until she had returned to her normal, real world.

"I think I'll look for a book full of romance. Any suggestions?" Mrs. Carson asked, interrupting Samantha's thoughts.

Yes, memoirs of her trip to the jungle, Samantha was tempted to say, remembering herself standing with Brock at the waterfall, embracing, kissing. The raw beauty of the Amazon had been reflected in the raw emotions between them. "Try this one," she finally answered, taking a new romantic saga off the shelf in front of her. She hadn't read it, but several of her customers had enjoyed it. Before, she would never have thought to recommend a book she hadn't personally read, but like other things in her life since the Amazon, that had changed too.

Mrs. Carson read the back cover, flipped through the first pages of the book, and said, "Thanks. I think I will. I've been so busy this last month that I haven't had a chance to ask you how your vacation was last month. Nell told me you went south."

"It was a change of pace."

"Your vacation must be different from the

ones I take. Whenever Tom and I go anywhere, we always end up running ourselves ragged, trying to see everything. We have to come home just to recuperate. I'm glad yours was quiet and peaceful."

Samantha smothered her laugh, turning away to act as if she were interested in stocking her shelves.

"Where did you go? Nell never said."

"Brazil."

"Ah, the warm beaches of Rio. I can see why you were rested. Did you sample any of the nightlife? I've heard it's quite hot."

Hot? Yes, it certainly was, Samantha thought, recalling the passionate nights spent in Brock's arms. "No, I rarely left my—accommodations."

"Oh. Well, that must account for all the rest you got. I'd better let you get back to work. I think I'll look around some more. This may be a two-book business trip."

Samantha paid little attention to the books she was placing on the shelves. Usually she loved to scan them, deciding which ones she would read first. But now when she went home at night she would end up daydreaming about another time, another place, another life. She no longer read or did the things she had done in her free time before the Amazon, before Brock.

Face it, Samantha Prince, you are bored and

lonely. You miss Brock, and no matter what you do, that fact isn't going to change.

She was beginning to think there was more of her brother in her than she had ever thought possible. Samantha was actually yearning for the life she had had with Brock. No, she was actually yearning for the man. She loved him, and nothing was going to change that—not time, not distance.

"Samantha, look at this!" Nell scurried over to her, waving a current news magazine at her. "There's an article about Mark in here."

"You're kidding." Samantha took the magazine and flipped through it until she found the article on her brother and the large gold deposit he had discovered.

But what riveted her attention was that next to Mark in the picture was Brock. Her heart stopped beating for a few seconds. She caressed the black-and-white image on the paper, wishing he were standing in front of her so she could caress the man.

"It tells all about how your brother found that man who was wounded and trying to escape the Major in the jungle. It makes Mark sound like such a romantic hero, describing how he tried to save the man's life, even though in the end the man died of an infection."

The prospector had been staying at the Major's outpost and had gotten drunk one night, telling them about the gold deposit he had found. From then on he had been running for his life. When Mark had tried to help him and the prospector had known he would die anyway, he had given Mark the complicated location of the gold deposit on the promise that her brother would make sure his wife back in Santarém was taken care of. Mark had written the directions down in his journal in his abbreviated code when he had realized he was in as much danger as the prospector had been.

"Who's the man in the picture with Mark? Is that the man who helped you?"

Samantha nodded, not trusting her voice. She hadn't told Nell much about Brock, to her friend's disappointment.

"Oh, wow. And you were with him for two weeks? I'm surprised you even came home. He's something else."

"Yes, he is," Samantha murmured, giving the magazine back to Nell, feeling more depressed and discontented than before. While she was in the Amazon she had kept trying to discover who Brock was, when in actuality his background was unimportant. It was the man he was that was important, and every day they had been together he had revealed another facet of his personality.

"You never told me much about what happened in the jungle. Is it scary? Are there a lot of snakes? Bugs?"

"Yes. Yes. And yes," Samantha said with a laugh. "In fact, Brock saved my life when I had a close encounter with a fer-de-lance."

"I'd have died."

Not with Brock around, Samantha thought. She could endure a lot with him. With that realization she knew she could even endure an uncertain future if Brock was a part of that future.

The ringing phone interrupted Nell's next question, and Samantha hurried to answer it. She was expecting Mark to call her today.

"Hi, Sam. How's everything?" Mark greeted her.

"More to the point, how are you doing? Any problems?"

"Not now. I just can't believe all the attention this thing is getting."

"I know. I saw an article on you in a magazine."

"A publisher has approached me about doing a book on my little escapade. What do you think? You're the book expert."

"It definitely has possibilities. You always were creative, Mark."

"I might, once things settle down."

Samantha laughed. "Settle down around you?"

"Sis, sometimes I envy your quiet, normal life."

And sometimes she envied his exciting, carefree life, she thought. Maybe that was the reason she always read adventures, thrillers, romances. "Listen, Mark Prince, things can get pretty exciting around here. I don't know if you could handle it. Just last week I had two checks bounce."

Her brother chuckled. "I hope to be in New Orleans in a month. Will you fix your favorite brother his favorite meal?"

"I'll fix my only brother shrimp gumbo."

"My mouth's watering just thinking about it. Till then, Sis."

"Wait. Mark—" Samantha started to ask her brother about Brock but wasn't quite sure what to ask. Brock had walked away from a long-term commitment in Manaus as much as she had.

"Brock was fine the last time I saw him. I kept your promise of ten percent. Hell, I'd have given the man half. He saved your life. But he only wanted the ten. He said something about an oil deal he needed to finish up. I haven't seen him in over a week. I wasn't going to ask, Sam, but you know your nosy brother. What happened between you two?"

"Nothing a plane ticket can't fix. Do you think he's still in Manaus?" She had changed Brock Slader's mind about helping her find Mark; she was determined to change his mind about a more important matter.

"I don't know. I can ask around. Why?"

"Because I'm coming to Manaus tomorrow."

"Samantha Prince, you aren't an impulsive person. What's this world coming to?"

"My world is finally going to be right. I'll see you tomorrow. See if you can track down Brock. You know me and the language."

"Yes, Brock told me about how you two met." Mark's laughter flowed over the line. "See you tomorrow, then."

With her decision made Samantha knew she had little time before she had to leave. First, she made a call to the airlines to book passage to Brazil. Then she informed Nell she was leaving again. Nell just smiled and told her that she had been expecting her to, especially after seeing the picture in the magazine. Samantha would have been crazy to let someone like him go, Nell informed her.

Standing behind the counter, Samantha tried to make a list of everything she needed to do in the next twenty hours. She was down to paying her bills when Mrs. Carson came to the register to pay for three books. Nell was busy stocking the shelves, so Samantha rang up Mrs. Carson's purchases, trying to hurry so she could leave.

The bell over the door rang, indicating another customer. It would be just her luck to have the busiest day of the year when she had to go home and prepare for her early-morning flight. Oh, well, it looked like another sleepless night. She was too excited to sleep anyway.

"Be right with you," Samantha automatically said to the customer who entered the store.

"Take your time, Sam."

Samantha spun about, dropped the change she was going to give Mrs. Carson, and stared at Brock. Mrs. Carson looked from Samantha to Brock, then back to Samantha.

"Is anything wrong, Samantha?" Mrs. Carson asked, worried.

Samantha shook her head, absently scooping up the money on the counter to hand Mrs. Carson. If the older woman hadn't quickly placed her hand under Samantha's, she would have dropped the change again.

"I was just talking to Mark," Samantha murmured, marveling at her ability to say something so unimportant when the occasion called for brilliance. This was her chance to convince Brock they could work everything out, and her mind was blank!

One corner of Brock's mouth lifted in a smile. "Is that any way to greet your knight after he's traveled thousands of miles to see you?"

A broad smile spread across Samantha's features as she rounded the counter and was across the store so quickly that Mrs. Carson was left wondering what had gotten into the sensible Samantha Prince.

Samantha threw her arms around Brock's neck and he lifted her off the floor, swinging her around and around.

"Oh, how I've missed you," she exclaimed.

He settled her back down on the floor, held her head in his hands, and kissed her soundly on the mouth. "And I've missed you, Samantha."

Mrs. Carson discreetly coughed, and Samantha blushed. She turned to her longtime customer and said, "Mrs. Carson, this is Brock Slader. I met him in Brazil."

"I'm glad to meet you. Thanks, Samantha, for the recommendation. I'll see you when I get back from my trip." As Mrs. Carson left the store, she gave Samantha a look that said she understood why Samantha had hardly left her accommodations.

Another customer came into the store only seconds after Mrs. Carson left. Brock whispered, "Do you have an office? Someplace we can go for privacy."

"The back room."

The second the door to the back room closed behind them, Brock drew her into his arms and kissed her over and over, as if he couldn't get enough.

"I've come to several conclusions in the last six weeks, Samantha. The first is that I love you and can't live without you. Will you marry me?"

"I never could accuse you of subtlety. Yes, I'll marry you. I came to the same conclusion. Do you think that's something we have in common?"

"I do know one thing we have in common."

"Oh, and what's that?"

"This." He pulled her close as his lips took hers in a kiss full of longing and love.

When Samantha could think and breathe again, she asked, "What is the other conclusion you came to?"

"I opened an IRA with some of the money from the gold deposit."

Samantha's eyes widened. "You? An IRA?"

He nodded.

One part of her was disappointed. It obviously meant he intended to stay in the States and try her life-style. She had just spent the last six weeks convincing herself that she wanted, even yearned, for his life-style. She would go anywhere, do anything, for Brock as long as they could be together.

"Well," she said, "I realize there was a certain thrill to the danger we experienced in the Amazon, but I think I can settle down to a sedate life as a suburban housewife if that's what you really want."

Brock tossed back his head and laughed. "Who said your life will be sedate? I may have opened a retirement plan to satisfy your need for security, but I'm leaving for Africa next month and I'm taking you with me."

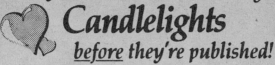